They're Not Strangers

It's A Vibe: Book II

By: J.D. Southwell

Dedication

To all my book-loving, unhinged, smutty book baddies

They're Not Strangers

Copyright © 2024 by J.D. Southwell.

All rights reserved. Printed in the United States of America. No part of this book may be used or reproduced in any manner whatsoever without written permission except in the case of brief quotations em- bodied in critical articles or reviews.

This book is a work of fiction. Names, characters, businesses, organizations, places, events and incidents either are the product of the author's imagination or are used fictitiously. Any resemblance to actual persons, living or dead, events, or locales is entirely coincidental.

For information contact :

Jd.southwell@outlook.com

http://www.jbookcollections.com

Book and Cover design by J.D. Southwell utilizing Canva

First Edition: June 2024

10 9 8 7 6 5 4 3 2 1

Also by J.D. Southwell

Dating is Ghetto

It's A Vibe Series

40hrs With A Stranger

Note to reader:

This story contains content that might be troubling to some readers, including, but not limited to, childhood trauma, abuse, attempted sexual assault, violence, kidnapping, slut shaming, anxiety, sexually explicit scenes, stalking, violence, and murder.

Name Pronunciation:

Akeno (a.kee.no)

Seojun (s.oh.j.un)

Chul-Moo (ch.ol – moo)

Chapter 1

Denice

One thing that I've learned over the years about myself is that you're not about to fuck over the people I care about and think you're going to get away with it. Ashlynn was my best friend, hell she was like a sister to me, but she was too damn sweet. Don't get me wrong, I love her, but that sweet shit was only going to get you so far.

I patiently waited in the parking lot of Kitty's, a nude strip club downtown, and checked my watch. Any minute that bitch would be strolling out, and I had something for her ass. If Ashlynn knew why I would be late for our biweekly game night, she'd have a fit. Then she'd send Nick's ass over here and have him try to drag me out of this parking lot. Ashlynn hated violence and confrontation, but that was okay – that's why I was present in her life. Hell, she should be thankful that I waited this long before ambushing this bitch.

I ducked behind a car when I heard the employee door swing open. A slight grin formed at the corner of my lips as I watched Kendra come waltzing out with her arm wrapped around some woman's waist.

"I know how to make you feel good, baby – you just wait and see what I can do with this tongue," Kendra slurred loudly.

"For what I'm paying, you fucking better," the other woman laughed.

I frowned as they walked past the car I was hiding behind. Kendra was still up to her nasty, hoe-ish ways. They reached Kendra's car, and I made my move. Quickly and quietly, I left my hiding spot and walked behind the pair. I snatched Kendra by the back of her neck and flung her down to the ground.

"Yo, what the fuck?" the other woman shouted.

"Get the fuck out of here before I beat your ass, too," I spat, kicking Kendra in her side.

"Dee, get the fuck away from me," Kendra grunted.

When I saw that the other woman hadn't budged from her spot, I raised my fist to her, disregarding Kendra's protest. She didn't hesitate to turn on her heels and return to the club, leaving her 'date' to defend herself. I turned to Kendra, but her hand skated across my face with a hard slap before I realized what was happening. My head snapped to the side, and pain shot across my cheek.

"You crazy bitch!" she yelled.

She cocked her hand back in an attempt to hit me again, but I dodged her. She stumbled, and I caught her chin with a quick two-piece jab. She fell backward with a grunt as she held onto her chin.

I wasn't done with her bitch ass yet and proceeded to get on top of her. I punched her again, causing blood to shoot out of her mouth.

"That's for Ashlynn," I snarled. I raised my fist and punched her one more time. "That was for me."

I got up and dusted myself off as I glared down at her. She lay there crying, but I had little remorse for her trifling ass. My phone buzzed in my back pocket, and I saw Ashlynn calling me.

"Let this be a lesson – keep fucking with people if you want to." I turned on my heels as I answered the phone. "Hey, love. I promise I am on my way."

"Girl, don't make me pull up on you," Ashlynn huffed through the phone.

"I just had to handle some business. Give me less than an hour, and I'll be there."

"Better be! Love you, bye."

"Love you too," I chuckled through the phone before disconnecting the call. I looked down at Kendra, who was still on the ground but glowering up at me. Hate radiated off of her, but I didn't give a fuck. I dared her to do something, but she didn't move. I scoffed before turning on my heels and back to my car.

I raced home, showered, and changed my simple black hoodie and blue jeans into a burgundy dress and black sweater. It was early spring, and while the air was warmer during the day, it was still cold at night.

I ran my hands down the snug fabric that highlighted my size sixteen body. Some people may have turned their noses at how tight the dress fitted me, especially around my cushy stomach, but I had no shame in my game. I knew I looked good, and I could steal a bitch man if I wanted to. Don't get it twisted, though; I'm nobody's side piece – I'm the main entrée. I just had no problem shutting a bitch down, especially when she wanted to be funny with the fat jokes.

Ashlynn used to tell me how much she loved my confidence, and I constantly reminded her that she could be the same way. As much as I loved her, she cared way too much about what a muthafucka had to say.

When I found out what she was doing to herself because of the dumb shit spewing out of her bitch ass ex-fiancé mouth and even her dad, I was ready to throw hands. I knew Kendra was saying slick shit, but those two assholes were about to feel my wrath. Luckily, Bobby got the boot, and Ashlynn's dad did everything he could to make things right.

I pulled on my thigh-high boots before fluffing out my natural curls and applying a coat of matching red lip gloss to my full lips. I debated applying a bit of makeup but thought against it. I didn't want to overdo it, and besides, I only planned to be there for a few hours. Knowing Ashlynn and Nick, they definitely invited Akeno, aka Ayzo, over, and I did not want to have to spend time with him longer than I had to.

My clit pulsed with the mere thought of him, causing me to clench my thighs together.

"Hell, no trick," I shouted at my pussy. "We're not doing that again. We just can't." I swallowed and took a deep breath before grabbing my car keys and heading out the door.

Chapter 2

Ayzo

I raised my fist to knock on Nick's apartment door but froze. It's not that I didn't want to hang out with my best friend. I missed two years of Nick's life and planned to make it up to him. It's not like I had a problem with Ashlynn - she was a damn sweetheart. I was ecstatic that the pair found each other in this ridiculous world, and I wanted them to be happy.

I hesitated because Denice was the one other person I knew would be here tonight. She's the woman who had a piece of my heart but didn't want anything to do with me. I knew she would be mine when we were sixteen, but things happened, and I failed her.

I thought I'd never see her again, but fate brought us back together. Unfortunately, she hates my guts now.

After everything that has happened over the past six months, my interactions with Denice have been brief and curt. Aside from the biweekly game nights we had with Ashlynn and Nick, she refused to be anywhere around me. Hell, they low-key just started game night a month ago because of how uncomfortable they were whenever Denice, and I were in the same room together. Talk about tension.

"Are you going to stand there looking like a dumbass with your hand in the air, or are you going to knock?"

I turned around to see Denice standing at the top of the stairs with her hands on her hips. I tried not to stare, but fuck she was looking good in that tight-ass red dress that made her full-bodied DDD breast pop out with long black boots that stopped at the top of her thighs. I licked my lips as I grinned at her, but she rolled her eyes and walked up to the door to knock.

"How are you doing this evening, Dee?"

"It's Denice and fine," she said, wrapping at the door.

I chuckled and leaned against the wall next to her. My eyes landed on her ass and gotdamn – her booty was quicker than quicksand and had me falling in fast. I instantly felt my dick jump.

"What the hell are you looking at, Akeno?"

I swallowed and contemplated my words. I couldn't flat out and say 'all that ass,' but at the same time, I didn't want to lie.

"I thought I told you to call me Ayzo – all my friends do."

"I am not your friend, and you are not mine. So, Akeno, I'll ask you again: what the hell are you looking at?"

By the way she clenched her jaw, I knew she was getting impatient, but seeing her mad turned me on.

"You, uh, are not the same girl I hung out with eight years ago," I stammered.

"Well, no shit! We were just teenagers, and I'm a grown-ass woman now."

"I only meant that you've grown into a beautiful, sexy woman. I mean, you were fine when we were younger, but damn, baby. Time has been doing you good."

She dragged her tongue across her teeth before turning toward me and giving me a sly, seductive smile. She ran her hand up my arm and batted her long eyelashes at me. My breath caught in my throat as she leaned toward me, allowing her lips to brush against my ear. Oh fuck she smelt good.

"Akeno?"

"Yeah?" I said in a breathy voice.

"Go fuck yourself. Respectfully."

She stepped away with her middle finger in my face as she rolled her eyes. A mixture of astonishment and humor crept through my body as I laughed throatily. She may have grown into this breathtaking woman, but she was still the same feisty girl I fell for all those years ago.

I opened my mouth, but the door flew open, and Ashlynn wrapped her arms around her friend. Nick followed behind and dabbed me up as we walked into the apartment. Taking off my coat, I admired my friend's new place.

The cozy two-bedroom, two-bathroom townhouse was decorated in a modern style with earthy-tone colors. The living room had a beige sectional couch and a matching lazy boy. In the middle of the living room was a glass coffee table piled with board games.

To the immediate left of the living room were double doors that led to the balcony patio, which had a magnificent view of the city.

What I'd give for a chance to wrap my hands around Denice's throat as I ate her out under the stars on that balcony. I'd gladly bend her over the rail and fuck her so good that everyone in the city knew what my name was. I chewed on my bottom lip and briefly closed my eyes. I needed to have patience, but her ass was going to be mine.

I walked past the dining area just off the living room and toward the kitchen, where I saw Ashlynn pouring everyone a shot of Jack Daniels. I arched an eyebrow at Nick and then at her.

"So, you a brown girl?" I asked, taking one of the shots. I honestly didn't even know that you drank. Every time I've seen you over the past few months, you've only had a water bottle.

"First, hell yeah, I drink! If it isn't brown, then I frown - clear liquor makes me feel sick. Besides, I've been helping Nick with not overindulging on his alcohol intake while I have been trying to drink more water. We agreed to only drink during game night or special occasions." Ashlynn stated.

"I can still have my beer, though," Nick chuckled.

"Nothing wrong with trying to break old habits in order to get healthy – I'm proud of y'all." Denice chimed in.

"Amen to that," I added. Our eyes briefly met before she quickly turned away when Ashlynn called her name.

"Denice, remember when we tried Everclear for the first time our freshman year?"

"Oh lawd! Don't remind me of that horrific night."

We clinked our glasses together and downed our drinks. I let the delicious burn run down my chest before letting out a growl.

"What happened?" Nick asked.

"It's too embarrassing," Ashlynn said, shaking her head.

"C'mon, bae – tell me," Nick said, wrapping his arms around her waist.

"Okay, okay, but don't you dare laugh. So, we were hanging out with a few of the older girls in our dorm, and I made the mistake of thinking that there wasn't any alcohol in the drinks after they told us it was there. Now, they liked to tease us first-year students and always played that trick on us."

"You'd be surprised how many girls were pretending to be drunk for attention," Denice stated.

"Exactly! Besides, you couldn't even taste it! So, I thought they were doing the same schtick, and I encouraged Denice to drink with me."

"And like a dumbass, I did."

"After the third cup, I couldn't feel my damn kneecaps."

"Ashlynn's ass was walking around ready to fight a few girls because she thought they stole her underwear."

Nick choked on his drink as he tried to stifle his laugh. "They stole what now?"

Denice burst out laughing. "Her panties! Ashlynn was storming up and down the hall, yelling she was going to beat every bitch ass in there who was sniffing her underwear."

"Hey! You were right there with me about to swing on every single female."

"Damn right! You're my sister – I've always got your back."

"Why the heck did you think somebody stole your underwear?" I asked, holding my side from laughing.

Ashlynn chuckled and shrugged her shoulders. "I have no idea. No one but Denice and Kendra had been in my room."

Denice made a disgusted face at the mention of Kendra's name. I stared at her as she rubbed her hand along her knuckles. If I didn't know any better, her hand seemed red with cuts on it. Denice quickly moved her hand out of view as we locked eyes. What the hell happened to her? I opened my mouth to ask, but she quickly excused herself with an excuse that she had to check some emails before she stepped outside onto the balcony.

"So," Ashlynn said, staring at me. "What's up with you two?"

"Wh-what you mean?" I asked, breaking my trance from watching Denice.

"Don't play dumb. There's some crazy tension between you two."

"Yeah, man – we've been best friends for a minute, and I know when someone has your interests. Besides, all you do is keep a shit load of secrets from me," Nick scoffed.

I grimaced as guilt washed over me. Nick was right; he and I were best friends, but he knew nothing about me except for the basic things I told him. I kept my past locked away from the world for years, hoping to bury it with me when it was time for me to leave this earth.

I gave him an apologetic smile, "I'll tell you everything one day. As for Denice and me, I messed up, and now that she's around, I have a chance to make things right."

I grabbed my drink and followed after Denice. I knew she and Ashlynn were close, and I figured she'd tell her what happened when she was ready. Unfortunately, it would turn me into the villain, and until I could recap the whole story, I'd be the bad guy – for her.

I had to get back into Denice's good graces. There was a lot of shit that happened eight years ago, but the only thing she knew was that I left her when she was most vulnerable. I didn't know how but knew I had to fix it.

I walked to the balcony door and watched Denice enjoying the cool spring air. I took a deep breath and opened the door. Her body stiffened as she took another sip of her drink.

"Why must you continue trying to bulldoze your way back into my life?" She said, not bothering to turn around.

"Are we never going to talk about what happened?"

"What is there to talk about? You left me after you got what you wanted – end of story."

"No, that's not the end of the story!" I argued, running my hands through my coils and down my face.

Denice dropped her head and puffed out her breath before gradually shifting to face me. She folded her arms across her chest and glared as she waited. I didn't know where to begin. What if I did tell her everything? That wouldn't mean she'd believe me. Hell, as much shit as I have been in, I wouldn't even consider myself to be truthful.

I opened and balled my fist. I desperately wanted another drink as my mouth became dry. The silence became deafening as I stood there like an idiot. *Just open your damn mouth and talk!* I shouted to myself, but I didn't. I was afraid. Afraid of how crazy I was about to sound.

Denice rolled her eyes and aggressively threw her hands up in the air. She gulped down the last of her drink before bumping past me.

"Fuck," I said under my breath, letting out a frustrated sigh.

I heard the door open before Denice spoke up. "I couldn't agree more."

I gripped the balcony railing and cursed. I wanted to explain myself to Denice, but how? Where would I even begin to describe everything that happened back then? Those few days were such a roller coaster of buffoonery that I doubt she'll believe me. I took a deep breath as I allowed the memories to flash through my mind.

Part 1
8 years ago

Chapter 3

Denice

I coughed on the pungent odor of the freshly lit blunt that was being actively passed between my ex, Luther, and his homeboy, Xavier. Once it was my turn, I froze.

"Here, Dee – take a hit," Luther urged.

When they said peer pressure was a bitch, they were not lying. The stern look on his face almost had me reaching for the blunt. Almost. I had no desire to smoke weed, especially since I watched Xavier lick all over the cigar to keep it closed while he rolled it. I had no idea where that fool's mouth had been, yet they expected me to put my lips on it voluntarily. Yuck – pass!

"I'm good," I said, averting my eyes from Luther's frown.

"Shorty lame as fuck," Xavier laughed as he took the blunt back.

"So what? Who's going to beat my ass?" I shot back.

Luther's face brightened as he burst out laughing. He clapped his friend on the back, "I tried to warn you, Dee, don't fuck around. When she doesn't want to do something, trust me, she ain't going to do it."

Xavier smacked his lips and waved a hand at me as he passed the blunt to Luther. I smirked at him before leaning back to examine the pair.

Xavier was barely 5'7 and swore up and down that he was black. Poor baby was white as milk with blonde hair and deep cobalt eyes. Not that I cared what he looked like, but in my opinion, he was trying too hard to fit in. He was cool as hell when he was just himself.

On the other hand, Luther was six feet tall with short black hair cut into a neat fade. His dark espresso skin was painted with tattoos across his arms and upper chest. He was a defensive lineman for his high school before he graduated last year, which explained his wide, thickset frame.

I had to admit Luther was fine as hell, and at times I felt lucky to have his attention. Especially since he was three years older than me, but he was too damn pretentious. He walked around like his shit didn't stink and every woman wanted him.

It was early August, and we were hanging out at the park, sitting on a bench. The sweltering heat in Chicago had nothing on what I was used to back in Houston, but it was all the same. I was hot as hell and wanted to go back home to soak my ass in a tub, but when Luther called, I came running.

Don't get it twisted - I would have told his ass to fuck off in a blink of an eye, but my foster sister was getting on my nerves. Plus, I was bored as hell just sitting in my room.

I sighed and tilted my head back. I missed Houston. I missed my home and my life before everything got turned upside down. I was making do with the hand I was dealt, but I was still pissed off. I never wanted to be thrown into the system and have to move in with new parents – let alone from Houston to Chicago. Dad Erin and Mama Julia have been excellent to me, but I missed my birth parents. Well, I missed them before the shit show happened.

"Yo, Dee," Luther said, slapping my thigh. His hand briefly lingered before he began to squeeze my legs. "How about we take a ride? Give you a chance to explore the city more."

I snapped my head upright and glared at him before pushing his hand away. "Luther, you are not slick. I am not about to get in the backseat with you no time soon."

"What must I do to make you my girl again?"

I huffed out a hearty laugh. "Oh please, Luther! You were my boyfriend for three days before I realized what type of guy you were. You are not one to be tied down to just one girl, and I don't want to hold you back. Besides, we are better as friends."

"Which is bullshit. We both like each other, yet you are fighting your feelings for me. I can't help that other girls flirt with me. Plus, I think you're just frontin'. I reckon you are just scared because you want to explore our sexual creativities together just as much as I do."

I arched a brow at him and cocked my head to the side before I fell out laughing. This fool could not be serious. Did he really think I was one of those gullible girls that ate up bullshit lies for some attention? Hell no!

"Nice try," I said, brushing a tear from my eye.

"C'mon now, baby! Let me prove how much you mean to me - let me just put the tip in so I can see how you feel," he said, whispering into my ear before biting down on my neck.

I briefly closed my eyes, relishing his lips on my most sensitive spot, but quickly pushed him away. "We've already been through this, Luther. I'm not having sex with you."

He smacked his lips and rolled his eyes. I shrugged and told him I'd see him later before walking away. I took my earbuds out and placed them in my ear. I made sure my music playlist was on a random shuffle as I headed toward my house. The smooth melodies of one of my favorite R&B songs came on, and I couldn't help but smile.

As much as I liked Luther, I wouldn't be his girlfriend again. I, for damn sure, was not about to give him my virginity, either. Just because we hung out and flirted now and then didn't mean I was obligated to allow him to label me as his and spread my legs for him. It's not like I thought about it, but I didn't trust him.

When I moved to Chicago, I saw how he toyed and interacted with the other girls on my block—always teasing and touching. I vowed to stay away from him, but his ass was smooth. One minute I was avoiding any path that he was on; the next, he was whispering the right shit in my ear. Pathetic, I know, but he was chill company when he wasn't trying to fuck. I didn't see any harm in hanging out with him until I made more friends.

Besides, I had no plans to be in any relationship. I didn't believe in love—it was for the weak, and it could be deadly. The soul-wrenching, can't eat, can't sleep, can't breathe without them type of love could easily have someone throwing logic out the window.

I scoffed as I walked past a couple kissing on the swing set. What did Tina Turner use to sing about love? It was a second-hand emotion. I personally saw the effects of someone loving too hard, and I vowed never to put myself in that position. I didn't care how much they so-called loved me.

Chapter 4

Ayzo

I tapped my fingers against the wooden desktop and tried to keep my eyes open. I get that it was the summer, but this damn classroom did not have to be this cold. How did they expect me to stay awake when I was freezing, comfortable, and the only one in the room? It was the perfect combination to doze off to sleep.

As much as I hated coming to summer school, I was willing to sacrifice a few hours of my day to ensure I graduated on time. I spent the past few years doing everything but worrying about school. My narrow head ass was skipping like a muthafucka, and my family could have cared less. As long as I was bringing in bread, someone behind the scenes guaranteed my grades were high enough to pass.

After a while, I realized I was not too fond of missing school. I didn't want someone my mom hired to manipulate the system so that I would barely pass. I know I couldn't make my bread by sitting in a classroom learning about half-truths when it came to our history or other subjects I'd hardly use in real life. Still, I didn't want to have my diploma based on lies. So, I told my mom to allow me to pass my classes independently.

"Akeno, can you please come to my desk?" Mr. Brown asked, walking into the room.

I rolled my eyes and got up from my desk. "Yo, Mr. B, I told you a hundred times that my friends call me Ayzo."

"And I told YOU a hundred times, I'm not one of your friends."

"Dang, I thought we were cool. I have been your favorite student all summer."

"You've been my only student all summer, and we are cool, but I'm a grown-ass man. What do I look like having a sixteen-year-old friend?" He laughed out loud.

"Hey! I'll be seventeen soon."

"Anyway, I just wanted to show you something."

I stepped around his desk as he clicked on a few tabs on his laptop. He pulled up my grades and paused. I squinted my eyes and tilted my head to the side. After blinking a few times and confirming my eyes weren't playing tricks on me, I looked at my teacher. I couldn't help the broad smile spreading across my face as I saw all A's and one B minus on my report card.

"Do you have the right person pulled up, Mr. B?"

He laughed, "I don't know too many students named Akeno Yi. You have really turned your attitude towards school around. You've gone from a D+ average student to an A- for your sophomore year. As long as you keep this up, you are on track to graduate on time and be at the top of your class. Colleges like to see things like that."

"Hell yeah!"

"Language, Akeno."

"My bad, sir," I said, covering my mouth.

Mr. Brown's stern look turned into a smirk after a few seconds. "Go, get out of here. I'll see you this fall, and I expect you to still have your head on straight. Your Junior year is not the time to be playing games."

"Yes, sir! See you around, Mr. B."

With that, I scooped up my backpack from my desk and dashed out the door. I was overjoyed that I was not only able to catch up on all of my schoolwork but that I actually passed with grades higher than C's. It's not like I was dumb, but like I said, I couldn't stack my money by sitting in a classroom. It may have been easier to let someone else keep doing the work for me, but that wasn't sitting right with me. I knew I had to handle my business and am glad I stuck with it.

I reached into my back pocket and grabbed my phone. It was a quarter until noon, and I still had the whole day to myself. I missed the chance to hang out with Luther and Xavier damn near all summer, so maybe they'd want to hang out today. Hell, it'd be the perfect way to celebrate.

I sent Luther a quick message asking if he wanted to smoke, knowing good damn well my ass didn't partake, but I knew that was the fastest way to get him to respond. He, of course, was down and told me to meet him at the park. I shoved my phone back into my pocket with a smirk.

After a few moments, I stepped inside my house and headed straight to my room to change my clothes. I did not want to linger longer than I had to. The cozy plum and gray color scheme around the house gave a false welcoming atmosphere, however, it was everything but. The décor that filled each nook and cranny would have made anyone feel at home as soon as they crossed the threshold, but it was my motivation to graduate and get as far away as possible.

I changed into a simple white tank and black basketball shorts. I tied my hair into a messy, curly bun and applied another coat of deodorant. I wasn't about to be caught smelling musty – it didn't matter how hot it was, niggas had no problem telling you about yourself, especially if you stunk.

I inspected myself in the mirror and grinned. The hair on my upper lip was starting to grow, finally allowing me to look my age. I was turning seventeen this winter, but my damn baby face made me look like I was still in middle school. Yeah, I was about 5'11, but many boys younger than me were the same height. So, I often blended in with the middle schoolers.

I rubbed a hand down my coffee-brown skin and thanked God that I didn't get too much acne during my higher puberty stages. I looked at my profile and scoffed. I had been working out and training for the past five years, but I was still skinny. Technically, I was muscular, but I wanted to get my weight up.

I chuckled to myself - I was being too critical for nothing. Most girls were all over me, and hell, who could blame them? I wasn't trying to be arrogant, but I had a full head of coiled curly hair, full lips, and soft hazel almond-shaped eyes. Plus, I was unique because most girls hadn't run into too many half-black and half-Asian kids before.

It was a new taste that they wanted to have, but I wasn't easy. None of the girls at my school or who I've seen around the city had gained my interest. I mean, I've fooled around with a few of them, but I never gave them my entire body. My friends called me lame, but I wanted my first time to be with someone special.

"What the hell are you doing here?"

I jumped and spun around to see my mom standing in the doorway. She wore black leggings and a pink crop top, highlighting her medium-golden complexion. Her long black hair, tied into a ponytail, swayed as she tilted her head to the side. Even though I towered over her five-foot petite statue, her deep brown piercing eyes glared into me, making me feel like I was the small four-year-old boy again.

"H-hey ma." The tight line her lips formed reminded me that I needed to answer her question now or else. "I was released early from school. Mr. Brown showed me my grades, and I am not only back on track to graduate on time, but if I keep it up, I could be at the top of my class academically."

She snorted before folding her arms. "It's not like you made the honor roll."

I quietly smacked my lips and grabbed a pair of shoes from the closet. I knew where this conversation was heading and wanted to get out of the danger zone as fast as possible.

"You know, if you would've stayed put and listened to me instead of trying to do things on your own, your stupid ass wouldn't even have to be in summer school. You'd be running your own territory without having to step foot in a classroom. You'd still pass all of your classes, but no. You'd rather work harder, not smarter, so that you could run around the neighborhood like a homeless rat," my mom said, pacing through my room.

"Omma." I sighed in her native tongue while placing my head in my hands.

"Don't, Mom, me, you worthless child," she spat back.

"What's the big deal? I want to get my diploma and maybe a degree the right way."

"Damn the right way! School should not be the priority. Continuing to work with your uncle and cousin to prepare to have your own territory should be at the top of your list."

"I don't want to do that.

"It's tradition!"

"No!" I snapped. "I've seen and done shit that was wrong with that fucked up so-called tradition, and I don't want any parts of it. If you want to be a part of that life so bad, then ask your brother to jump you back in."

I instantly regretted my words as fury spread across my mother's face. I bowed my head, "Mom, I'm sor –"

I briefly looked up and saw her small olive-complected knuckles approaching me and connecting with my jaw. I stumbled back and gripped my chin. My mom may have been a mere 110 pounds, but her hands were heavy as hell.

"This tradition is what keeps money in my pockets. It keeps food in your ungrateful mouth and is built on loyalty. What has a diploma and a college degree done for your worthless dad? Hired as an entry-level associate at a corporate job kissing ass for people who couldn't give a shit about him!"

"At least he's safe – not having to watch his step wherever he goes. He's not hurting innocent people! As I said, a fucked up tradition that only a fucked up person would enjoy," I seethe.

My head snapped to the side as my mother backhanded me. Her nostrils flared as she huffed out steams of breath. "Get the hell out – I don't want to look at your weak, pathetic face. While you're out, why don't you tell your cousin Seojun what you think about our tradition."

With that, she turned and stormed out of my room. I grabbed my phone and wallet before heading out the door. I didn't need this shit. Sometimes, I hated that woman. She spent years training and beating family traditions into me, but I didn't want that. I just wanted to be average – get my degree and live my life. I didn't want to be the Shadow anymore.

Chapter 5

Denice

I let out a frustrated breath as I reread the same sentence for the third time. I usually was the only one awake before seven in the morning and I liked to use the time to get through my TBRs – to be read. My bookshelf was piled with various genres, from young adult, Christian fiction, and novellas to the smuttiest, dark romance and fantasy novels that'll make you embarrassed to read them in public.

"What a man, what a man, what a man, what a mighty good man!" Mama Julia sang out at the top of her lungs.

I rolled my eyes. I get that it was my adoptive parent's house, but damn have some common courtesy that others might still be asleep. When I was up early, I stayed as noiseless as possible to enjoy the peace and quiet - not Mama Julia. She wanted everyone to know that she was awake. And by what and how she was singing, she wanted everyone to know she got dicked down pretty good last night. I could gag at the thought of my bonus parents getting freaky together.

Over the years, I quickly learned how Saturday mornings would be by the first song Mama played. If it was a slow and sad melody, I was in for some major deep cleaning followed by side remarks under Mama's breath whenever Dad Erin entered the room. Now, if the pace was fast and you could easily have danced to the beat, we would spend the morning eating good food and head out shopping afterward.

I chuckled as I set my book down next to me on the bed. I loved my adoptive parents and couldn't have been more blessed to be chosen by them. I didn't always think that way, though.

When I was eight years old, the police took me away and said I had to go into foster care. I was terrified. I was worried about being abused by the adults or other kids in the house. While I had never known anyone who had been in foster care, I had seen a lot of movies and documentaries with my mom about how destructive it could be for individuals.

God had his hand on me during that confusing time in my life. I was at the orphanage for less than twenty-four hours when I was told that I'd be placed into foster care with the lovely Hintson family. They assured me that I was going to be comfortable.

I remember the first time I met the Hintsons. I was sitting on a tiny chair in the hallway at the orphanage as the pair talked to the social worker. My heart pounded against my chest, and I continually rubbed my hands down my pant leg to remove the sweat. I stared at them, noticing that they were an interracial couple – she was black, and he was white. It was my first time seeing mixed couples, and I instantly noticed they seemed happy.

The first thing that caught my eye about Julia was her natural hair—it was just like mine. She noticed me staring at her hair and gave me a wink. A broad smile spread across her lips immediately, making me feel comforted. Her rich chocolate skin highlighted her beauty. Her deep brown eyes abruptly flashed with sympathy as she spoke with the childcare worker regarding what had happened to me. She gave me an affectionate look before she began signing the paperwork.

On the other hand, I could tell Erin was nervous by the deep shades of pink around his ears and down the back of his neck. He towered over Julia and the worker, standing at least six feet with dark chestnut hair. His piercing green eyes darted between his wife and the social worker before landing on me. He anxiously flashed a set of white teeth, the bottom row occupied with braces, before playfully sticking his tongue out and winking, causing me to giggle.

They didn't seem cruel, but I kept my guard up. My mom used to tell me growing up that just because people smiled in your face did not mean they wouldn't betray your trust. I remembered my stomach plunging as I swallowed the bile inching up my throat with the thought of my mother – my father. I wished I didn't have to be there. I wished that day had never transpired, but I couldn't turn back time.

A knock came at my door, breaking me out of my thoughts. I raised my eyes to see Olivia peeking her head through the door. Of course, she was awake, too. Ugh! I cocked an eyebrow at her and let my head drop back down as I picked up my book.

"Girl, all the blood is rushing to your head, and yet you are still trying to read upside down."

"I like reading like this," I murmured, stretching my legs against the wall.

"I guess, but you sound and look stupid."

I rolled my eyes but kept them on my book.

"Anyway," she continued, "will you miss me? I know y'all will, but it's okay to say it out loud."

I flipped over and sat upright in my bed. I looked at my temporary Latina foster sister with disbelief at her outright narcissism. Not only was I ecstatic that her selfish kleptomaniac ass was leaving, but I was damn near on the verge of doing backflips.

Olivia had moved in about six months ago, but her ass walked around here as if we owed her for allowing us to be in her presence. She bragged about how prettier she was because she was a Latina. Olivia ensured everyone knew how much longer her hair was, and it was effortless to detangle since it was just as curly as mine and Mom Julia's. She boasted about how skinny she was just because she was size four, but still had ample breasts, wide hips, and a plump ass that men wanted. Let me not forget my favorite brag from Olivia and how she could make anyone laugh. Bitch thought she was a stand-up comedian with her tired-ass jokes.

When she wasn't opening her arrogant trap, she was swiping money from Mama Julie's purse or Dad Erin's wallet. My adoptive parents knew what she was doing, too, but their big hearts only wanted to help her. They turned a blind eye to some things I thought were only enabling her. I, on the other hand, wasn't for that shit. I caught her ass going through my shit one time, and on that day, she learned how heavy my hands were.

I gave her a tight-lipped smile. "It sure will be quiet around here when you leave."

"Right! I would leave you some of my clothes that I don't want anymore, but you know, two different sizes."

I sucked on my teeth and grinned, "True because I actually grew into a woman's body when I hit puberty instead of looking like a Q-tip with hair and a few hips."

"You know, there is a difference between being sexy thick and just plain ole fat. Maybe you should look into that."

I stood up from my bed and balled my hands into fists. This bitch was asking to get one last beat down before her mom came and picked her up.

"Girls?" Mama Julia called before stepping into the room. The smile she had faltered as soon as she felt the tension. "Everything okay?"

"Of course, Julia!" Olivia chirped, exiting the room.

Mama Julia sighed as she slowly closed her eyes and shook her head. As fast as her frustration appeared, it quickly dissolved.

"Anyway, what are your plans for today, sweetie?"

I slumped back down on the bed. "I'm not sure. I might go hang out with Luther."

Mama Julia sucked her teeth before letting out a breath.

"Is that a problem?" I asked, already knowing the answer.

"Honey, I trust you, but I do not like nor trust that boy. I've seen him walking around here toying with every damn person that has tits and ass."

"Here we go," I groaned, dropping my head in my hands. It was too early for a lecture.

"I'm just saying. I was sixteen once upon a time, and I've been deceived by a pretty smile and charming lies."

"I know, I know. I may be young, but I'm not gullible. I don't like Luther like that – he's just nice to hang out with. Besides, when school starts, I'm pretty sure I'll meet some other people to hang out with and forget all about him."

"Alright, baby," she said, kissing me on top of the head. "With that said, can you be a dear and take Olivia with you after you're finished with Luther? I want her to have one more night of safe fun. Lord knows what she has to go through when her coked-out mom gets her back."

I raised my eyebrows and gave her a questioning look.

"Shit – sorry, baby. I know that poor girl didn't have much guidance growing up, and her mom literally only cares about her just enough until she gets her tax refund back. Then, she's back to her old ways. Makes me sick!"

Damn, poor Olivia. I had no idea what she was going through, but that didn't excuse her for being a dick to everybody. I've been through a real-life horror show myself, but I didn't use that as a clutch.

I exhaled and mumbled, "I'll offer an invitation, but I highly doubt she'd want to hang out with me."

"It's the thought that counts. Your dad and I are going out tonight and will be back late. The emergency numbers are on the fridge, and money for pizza is in my secret stash."

"Yes, yes, I know."

Mama Julia gave me another kiss on the forehead before practically skipping out of the room. Her giddy attitude was contagious, and I loved seeing her happy.

I sighed and picked up my book again. I guess it wouldn't hurt that Olivia hung out with me just for a few hours. Besides, after today, I wouldn't have to worry about her ass anymore.

Chapter 6

Ayzo

Luther, Xavier, and I wandered the city without a permanent destination. I was lowkey starting to get bored of moving from one location to another only to fire up a blunt or watch them try to pick up girls, but I hadn't hung out with my friends in a while. Plus, I was not trying to go back home with my mom still there. Even though I had been gone for twenty-four hours now, it still wasn't sufficient time to ensure my mom wasn't pissed off.

I sighed and leaned my head back, resting it on Luther's car roof with the thought of my mom. After years of her abusive outbursts, you'd think I'd be used to it. The pain wasn't as bad since I was damn near immune to it, but the fact that she put her hands on me still hurt.

From the moment she found out she was pregnant with me, she made it known that I was a mistake. Hell, you could even say that she damn near hated my existence. The one-night stand she had with my dad turned into a forced marriage due to the lack of money and the end of her freedom. Granted, she had a choice to either give birth and move in with her parents or marry my dad. My mother despised her parent's strict household, so she chose the latter.

Even though she had her freedom, she made it known that we were the last result. She bragged about how much she missed her life before meeting my dad, got stuck with us, and wished she could return in time.

My poor dad tried his hardest to keep her happy by buying her everything she wanted or doing whatever she asked. He explained to me how much she loved us, and she was just sad because she wasn't used to the new life of being a mom. Our duty was to keep her satisfied and content so that she would stay.

So, I did everything I thought would please her – household chores, cleaning, and getting good grades in school. Everything we did wasn't good enough, and one of us eventually was on the receiving end of my mother's fists as soon as she was pissed off. My dad usually stepped in and took all of her beatings, but sometimes, I was the punching bag.

When I was going to give up, my mom surprised me with a unique project on my tenth birthday. I was over the moon and ecstatic about rekindling our mother-son relationship. I hoped to rebuild our family, but little did I know what I was getting myself into.

"Yo, what you think about thicky over there?" Xavier asked, exhaling a large cloud of smoke and breaking me out of my thoughts.

"That's all mine," Luther exclaimed, jumping off the car's hood and cracking his neck.

"What about ole girl you had with us yesterday?"

"What girl?" I asked, lifting my head to stare at the pair.

"Just some new girl from Houston that moved on my block at the beginning of summer. You would've met her sooner if you weren't so pressed about attending summer school. She is not trying to let a nigga clap them cheeks, though, so I have every right to explore other options to satisfy my needs. I'm going to get her one day."

"My ninja!" Xavier laughed, dabbing him up.

I rolled my eyes and chuckled. Xavier ass said nigga one time, and Luther almost beat the brakes off his white ass. He was lucky I was there and stopped him, but Xavier made sure to say ninja from here on out.

"I'm about to grab a drink at the store; you want anything, B-rad?" I asked Xavier, referring to Jamie Kennedy's character from Malibu's Most Wanted.

"Fuck you!" Xavier said, throwing up his middle finger before rolling up another blunt. "I'm straight, though."

"I'm good," Luther said, staring at the same girl. "Yo ma, hold up!"

The tall espresso slender girl stopped to look over at us. She shyly smiled as Luther licked his lips. I recognized her from school and passed her in the halls a few times, but I didn't know who she was. What I did know was she was now a sophomore.

"Oh, Ayzo, don't worry about paying when you go into the store. If the owner gives you any lip, tell him it's for Luther – that'll set him straight." With that, Luther walked over to the girl and started working his magic.

What did he mean by 'set him straight'? I shook my head, ignoring his remark. I jogged across the street to the convenience store before looking over my shoulder. Luther was rolling the girl's hair in between his finger and thumb as she placed her number in his phone.

Luther must've been aiming for a world record regarding how many numbers he could get today. I wasn't hating, but damn. Half the girls he talked to were still in high school, like me. His ass needed to move around because it was lowkey getting creepy as fuck.

Luther was my oldest friend, but he tended to be persistent in the wrong set of goals. He was smart as hell, and it was scary how good he was at manipulating people to do what he wanted. Whether it was lying to females to get his dick wet or doing some crazy off-the-wall shit that could catch a nigga a case.

When I met up with my friend yesterday, he bragged about going on crime sprees by robbing, stealing, and intimidating people for money – hence the owner at this corner store giving him free shit. I had no idea where this type of behavior was coming from, but the shit was getting old fast. If he wanted to live his life like that, then I would move around.

Now, I'm no saint and have done my share of wrongdoings, but the difference between me and him was I didn't purposely get violent. Besides, no one knew of my sins. I loved my homeboy, but his dumb ass ran his mouth too much, and that's how you'd get caught.

Walking into the convenience store, I grabbed a bottle of water and a jumbo cup of ice. It was hot as fuck, and I damn near grabbed a bag of ice to keep in the car, but I wasn't about to be carrying it around all day.

I walked down the snack aisle and reached out to grab a bag of Funyuns when a hand bumped into mine, attempting to grasp the same bag.

"Shit, my bad." A delicate voice expressed.

"It's all good —" I started, but my words got caught in my throat.

I looked up to a set of light brown eyes and full lips. A timid smile briefly appeared before she quickly turned around and walked toward the next aisle. I shook my head, breaking my daze, and followed behind her, unable to keep my eyes off this breathtaking female.

Her creamy mocha skin glistened with small beads of sweat, causing her black tank top shirt to cling against her and show off her curvy body. Her voluptuous hips hugged her blue jean shorts, highlighting her thick thighs that I wanted to sink my teeth into. She was rocking her natural hair, which was pulled up into a wild bun on top of her head.

I dragged my bottom lip in between my teeth — baby girl was fine as fuck. Many guys my age wouldn't have given her a second glance because she was chubbier than most girls around here, but not me. I did not discriminate; attractive as she was, I would be a fool not to talk to her.

She looked over her shoulder and caught me gaping at her again. Fuck, I was looking like a whole stalker right now. I cleared my throat and pretended to examine the nutrient facts for a bag of pistachios.

"Real smooth," she laughed, walking past me.

"I'm Akeno, but everyone calls me Ayzo," I blurted out.

"Nice to meet you."

"Aren't you going to tell me your name?"

"Eh," she shrugged.

She handed her money to the clerk at the register before stepping out the door. What the hell? Her nonchalant attitude toward me caught me off guard because, typically, when I introduced myself to a girl, they were all over me - but this girl wasn't fazed. I could tell she wasn't about to swoon over my looks. Nah – she was different, and I was intrigued. I needed to keep it cool and casual with her.

I exhaled a nervous breath before giving the cashier a few bucks. He reluctantly took it after staring between me and out the front window. I assumed he was watching Luther. I dipped my chin as I put the money in his tip jar instead and assured him that if asked, I received everything for free. He nodded with appreciation.

I darted out the door and hoped to catch up with the mystery girl. Thankfully just a few feet away, she was taking a sip from her water bottle.

"What are you getting into today? Want to come hang out at the park across the road?" I rambled out. Well, hell. There goes my plan to stay composed and casual. I had no idea why I was acting jittery – no girl has ever made me feel this nervous.

A broad grin plastered on her face before she burst out laughing. "Ayzo, right? You're a bit eager, aren't you?"

I rubbed the back of my neck before laughing nervously. "My fault. I planned to come talk to you calmly, but uh, as you can see, I am failing miserably."

A giggle parted from her full lips and made butterflies glide in my stomach. "It's cute. I don't run into too many guys who still get nervous."

"Oh, they're nervous; they just hide it better than me."

"Well," she chuckled, "I like it when a guy shows me a little vulnerability instead of walking around like they are God's gift to women and can do no harm. Especially when they are nothing but an egotistical ass wipe."

I arched my eyebrow and stared at her. That was oddly specific.

"Boyfriend problems?" I asked. I held my breath as she huffed out a laugh.

She found it funny, but I was silently praying that she was single.

"I've been told that I can be a great listener."

"I don't have a boyfriend."

I tried to hold it back, but the smile at the corner of my lips fully appeared. "Is that right? So, I can get your number, and you'd be down to hang out with me?"

She blushed and grinned back at me. "Yeah, we can do that. By the way, I'm De -"

"Yo, Denice!"

Her body stiffened as Luther jogged towards us. I darted my eyes between her and my friend and frowned. Oh, hell nah! Was she one of Luther's groupies that he'd already run through? I wasn't judging her, but I refused to dig into another man's mine.

I've known Luther for a while, and I knew how territorial he was, and as fine as she was, I wasn't going to do my homie like that. But still, I couldn't help the scowl on my face as he wrapped his arm around her shoulder and planted a kiss on her temple.

"I was just about to text you, girl."

"Sure, you were," Denice said sarcastically, removing his arm from her shoulder and wiping the kiss he gave her away.

I noticed the disgusted face he gave her. What the hell was his problem? Then it hit me that Luther must've been the 'God's gift to women' ass wipe that she was referring to—a sense of relief washed over me. Finally, a girl around here that wasn't taking the bullshit spewing out of Luther's mouth. Don't get me wrong, he homie, but he said whatever he could to get in between a woman's legs.

Luther broke his scowl with a double-take and looked over at me. His face suddenly lit up. "Ayzo! Did you get everything you needed from the store.?"

"Yeah. I got some water and ice because it's hot as the devil's drawers out here – didn't pay a dime."

"Good. Wait, hol' up, were you over here trying to spit game at my girl?" He asked, laughing. "Sorry to break it to you, but she's mine."

Denice let out an appalled scoff before folding her arms across her chest. "Luther, calm down – we are not together anymore, and I wouldn't hold my breath with any chances that we'd rekindle anything in the future."

"You can deny it all you want, but you will be mine. Stop frontin' because one of my homeboys around."

She glared at him. "Whatever helps you sleep at night. Anyways!"

I smirked and looked over my shoulder as I tried not to laugh. Luther's face was scrunched up with anger and embarrassment. Yeah, I know it was messed up to laugh at my oldest friend, but Denice was not falling for any of his shit.

"So," I coughed in an attempt to change the subject, "this is the girl you were telling me about earlier?"

"Yes, sir! Dee, this is my homie Ayzo. His nerdy ass has been in summer school this whole damn time – missing all the fun."

"Nothing wrong with making your education a priority, Luther," Denice said, rolling her eyes. "Nice to meet you, Ayzo."

She extended her hand toward me, and I gladly accepted. She was so soft and delicate. I gazed at her, and for a brief moment, a hint of desire swirled in her eyes before she blinked and let go of my hand.

She averted her eyes as I smirked and nodded my head. So, this breathtaking, feisty temptress was called Denice. Sexy, funny, and bold – my type of woman. My smile faltered as Luther territorially stepped closer to her. I knew he already had his eyes on her, and like I said before, I didn't step on anybody's toes.

"So, what are we about to get into?" Denice asked, still glancing at me.

"Let's cruise around and see what we can find," Luther said, grabbing her hand. He attempted to pull her toward the car, but she motioned for him to proceed to the vehicle.

Luther rolled his eyes but quickly forgot about his annoyance when his phone chimed with a text message. A sly smile developed across his lips as he strode away. Denice shook her head at him before locking eyes with me.

"C'mon Ayzo, you can sit next to me."

I grinned and strolled next to her towards the car. She playfully nudged me, instantly filling my heart with the need for her affection. Damn, I wanted her on my arm, but Luther's ass was trying to add her to his roster. I knew for a fact that he didn't want anything from her but to dive in between her legs. Then again, I'd be lying if the thought wasn't in the back of my mind, too. Dammit, what the hell was I thinking?

I jerked my head, erasing the thought. I could handle hanging out with Denice and keeping my lustful thoughts to myself. I mean, she wasn't throwing herself at me like many other girls I've met or ones Luther usually kept around. Besides, knowing Luther, he was going to do everything in his power to get Denice alone with him, keeping me and Xavier away from her.

I inwardly shrugged. I wasn't going to try any slick shit and let my homeboy do his thing. Besides, I had to remember what my grandfather and dad taught me. I needed to save my purity until I found the woman who was worth it.

We made it to the car, and I could feel my pulse drumming against my chest. Denice was bent over, attempting to climb in the backseat – her ass snatching my entire attention. Shit, this was going to be tougher than I thought.

Chapter 7

Denice

I tried my hardest not to stare at Luther's friend, Ayzo, but fuck, he was fine. His seductive smile and nervousness around me had my body heating up. Damn it, why couldn't I have met him first? No, Luther and I weren't together, but I'd feel like some hussy if I dropped one friend to get with the other.

"What you over there thinking about?" Luther asked, shifting closer to me in the backseat.

I rolled my eyes. I wanted Ayzo to sit next to me while Luther and Xavier smoked, but of course, Luther had to bully his way to me, and for what? Because I had a pair of tits and a coochie, aka he thought he could tell me what I wanted to hear so he could get some. Dumbass.

"Denice, baby, you look delicious," he whispered as he buried his head in my neck.

My eyes glanced over at Ayzo, who briefly made eye contact with me from the mirror of the passenger visor. He quickly shut the mirror and looked out the window as I nudged Luther off of me. His dark eyes pierced through mine, and I shifted uneasily in my seat.

"It's too hot for you to be all over me like that. Anyways, I'm not thinking about anything."

He rolled his eyes and scooted back to his side of the car. "Yo, it's getting late, and I'm tired of sitting in this car. Let's drop Dee off back home and get fucked up. I can swipe one of my uncle's whisky bottles from his 'secret' cabinet."

My heart began hammering against my chest. I didn't want to go home yet. I didn't care that Luther was getting aggravated with me for not catching on to his attempt to swoon me. Honestly, I only got in the car to find a reason to hang out with Ayzo.

"Wait," I blurted out. "My folks usually go out Saturday nights and don't return until late Sunday afternoon. You can come to my place."

"Dee, no offense, but your house is probably dry as fuck. You don't smoke or drink, so I highly doubt your parents do." Xavier commented.

"First of all, nobody asked you. Second, they have a liquor cabinet – I'm pretty sure most adults do."

He nodded as he made a U-turn back toward my side of town. I grabbed my phone and shot Olivia a quick text message.

> Are you home?

> Depends

I puffed out a breath of annoyance and gripped the phone.

> I'm having company over

> Well Well Well

> They have weed

> ...

> I know all about your habits. I can't threaten to tell the Hintsons about your illicit hobby since you are leaving, but I know for a fact that you haven't had a blunt in a while. Why not indulge on your last night?

> Clever bitch. Okay, bring your company over. If the weed is good, I'll keep my mouth shut.

I grinned and bit the corner of my lip. "We're good to go. The other foster girl promised to stay quiet as long as the weed is adequate."

Xavier let out a hearty laugh. "She better put five on it."

Luther muttered something under his breath that sounded like 'or something else,' but he waved me off when I questioned him. I swear I was getting tired of his disrespectful ass.

Why did I even bother to keep entertaining him? I knew he had plenty of other girls to whisper charming lies to. Hell, he didn't think I saw him earlier when I was at the convenience store talking to some girl, but I did. I didn't care, but I saw.

I sat back in the seat and wondered why Luther even kept talking to me. I've repeatedly denied him access to my honey, but he faithfully texts me. To be fair, when none of his friends were around and it was just me and him, Luther was a completely different person.

He didn't care about sex or anything in the category. He was kind, and we could talk for hours about some real shit. Or, we'd sit in silence, enjoying each other's company. Sex would never even come up during those times, but as soon as Xavier or any other of his friends were around, he was back to his shenanigans. I didn't know what made him act that way, but I had no plans to keep him around as company for much longer, especially if I was able to get to know Ayzo more.

"Shoot me the address. I have to handle some business," Ayzo instructed as we pulled to a stop light. Before I knew it, he opened the passenger door and hopped out of the car.

What the hell?

Chapter 8

Ayzo

As much as I wanted to hang out with Denice, I knew if I didn't get my ass over to see my cousin, I'd be in more trouble than I already was. Knowing my mom, she would have already told on me about how disrespectful I was being yesterday, so I might as well deal with the consequences now before I got dragged in. Thankfully, my cousin Seojun wasn't as strict as my uncle when it came to discipline.

    I trekked up a couple of blocks from where I got out of Luther's car until the familiar black and purple graffiti caught my eye—Jaguar territory – my mother's true home. When I agreed to help my mom with her unique project all those years ago, I didn't know that it would alter my life.

She had introduced me to her brother, Chul-Moo, who dominated the area within a hundred-mile radius. He had drug dealers, pimps, dirty cops, and straight-up killers all working for him. He also collected rent from the local businesses in exchange for their protection from any rival gangs. Still, nobody was stupid enough to fuck with my uncle.

My cousin Seojun and I were groomed under my uncle's rule. He made arrangements with my mother to have Seojun take over the Jaguars while I helped to expand the territory to the East Coast. Seojun learned about the books and how to handle the day-to-day business with my uncle, while I learned how to be The Shadow.

I learned how to fight, blend in, and steal vital information from under people's noses. I was stealthy and fast—easily overlooked if you weren't paying attention to your surroundings. I became so good at what I did that my uncle sent me on missions for influential people.

I'm not talking about people with a few businesses under their name that had local popularity. I'm talking about people who worked for the government, those who had two commas in their bank accounts, and those who had too much to lose.

I had to admit that it was entertaining at first. I got a cut of the money, which my mom took, but it satisfied her. I liked seeing her happy, especially if I was the one who made her smile, but I quickly learned that her happiness came at a hefty price.

I started with small tasks—sneaking into places to grab documents off USB flash drives or taking pictures of people in compromising positions to use as blackmail. My uncle had other shadows like me, but I was the best. I was the first choice for all the jobs, and for a while, I was happy.

As I got older, I was assigned riskier and more dangerous tasks. That pushed me to train harder and never let my guard down.

I was lethal, but having to constantly watch my surroundings and look over my shoulders for potential danger was beginning to take a toll on me. I was just barely entering into puberty but feared I wouldn't make it to my next birthday.

One day, my uncle advised me that it was time I learned how to handle the more physical parts of the job. I remember arriving at a small bakery that had just opened. It was run by a young interracial couple in their late thirties. My uncle informed them about the mandatory dues for setting up a shop in his territory. However, they did not have the total amount to cover the dues when the time came.

My uncle instructed me to assist his 'landlord,' who was responsible for collecting rent from all tenants. When we got to the bakery, we had to rough them up.

I threw up that night after I left them bloodied and bruised. All of the amounts of training could not have prepared me to hear bone crunching in my ears - blood spilling from an innocent person at my hands. I decided then that I wanted out. It took me a while, but my Uncle Chul-Moo pardoned me from the Jaguars on my sixteenth birthday.

I vowed never to go back to that lifestyle. That's when I told my mother I wanted to complete school alone. My mother was pissed, but my uncle reassured me that if I ever changed my mind that I was more than welcome to come back. She did not like that and wanted me to stay with the Jaguars so that she could live the lifestyle she was used to, but that shit just wasn't for me.

Since my mom was a woman, she was not allowed to hold any type of powerful position within the Jaguars. If she wasn't working as one of the prostitutes, then she was confined in her spot as a housewife. My mother only had a say so in certain areas because I was The Shadow, but after I left, she lost access.

I opened the door to my cousin's office, disguised as a massage parlor. It was a perfect cover-up for his prostitutes to work without having to worry about the police officers who weren't on his payroll. Two of his bodyguards, dressed like regular customers so as not to cause suspicion, sat in the waiting area.

Standing around the receptionist desks were Cindy and Sandy, two Asian girls barely eighteen whom I grew up with. My uncle took them in from their doped-out parents and groomed them into his perfect obedient toys. I didn't know everything he made them go through, but I knew it couldn't have been good. My stomach churned with the mere thought of what they had to endure.

Sandy tossed her long black hair over her shoulder and rested her back against the desk. "Akeno, you are growing into such a tasty man," she purred. Her eyes hungrily took me in as she slowly licked her lips.

I ignored her and tried to walk past when Cindy stepped before me. I examined her and detected that her hair was pulled up into two blonde pigtails for clients who liked them a particular age. Her white shirt stopped just below her breast, and her skirt revealed her small ass cheeks.

"I bet he's grown into a man in multiple different places," she breathed, trailing her hand down my chest until she brushed the top of my shorts.

I quickly grasped her wrist and pushed her away. "Don't touch me – neither of you. Besides, yall act like we're not damn near the same age."

She giggled, "Akeno baby, you are still a child."

"Agreed. I bet you're still a virgin," Sandy chimed in. She dragged her hand across my back while wrapping her other arm around Cindy's waist. "We can help with that – free of charge."

My heart pounded as they each tried to run their hands up my arm or down my chest. I knew that I wanted nothing to do with them, but my traitorous dick was ready to try something else besides a hand. Little by little, I felt as if I was about to fail this fight.

"My little cousin is not one of our customers – I suggest you get your hands off him."

Seojun stood against the employee door with his arms folded across his chest. His jet black hair was pulled up into a man bun that showed off the Jaguar tattoo on his neck that he received on his fourteenth birthday – courtesy of becoming a man. He wore a black suit jacket without an undershirt, black slacks, and black loafers. Two gold chains hung from his neck, accompanied by the gold hoops in his ears.

He glared at the pair with his dark hazel eyes as they scattered back to their assigned desks, heads bowed. He finally looked at me and smiled, showing off two gold fangs. "Missed you, kid – c'mon."

I exhaled a breath of relief as the haze of lust cleared from my mind. I was another hand rub down my chest from allowing these two succubus to have their way.

"Aunt K called," Seojun stated. We had reached his office, and he was sitting in his seat behind his desk.

My lips slightly parted with an excuse to give for my behavior, but nothing came to thought. Seojun may have been my blood and older than me by four years, but he still had the authority to get rid of me at the snap of his fingers. I've seen countless family members fall to their deaths by Seojun because they double-crossed or disrespected him.

I squared my shoulders and stared into his eyes. "My mom must understand that I am growing to be my own man. I love her, but I have to learn on my own. I respect you and am grateful for everything Uncle has taught me, but I do not want to be the shadow."

"Because you think it's a fucked up tradition?" Seojun taunted back.

I winced as the words I spat at my mother came back to slap me in the mouth. I bowed my head and took in a breath. "I apologize; it was said out of anger."

"But do you think it's true? I mean, about our traditions?"

"When it comes to harming innocent people for money, yes." I boldly stated.

My cousin's eyebrows shot up to his hairline as he gaped at me. My body tensed under his glare, but I did not avoid his eye contact. I wanted him and my mother to know my seriousness about escaping this lifestyle. I didn't want to end up in the grave before I graduated high school because of the dangerous situations I was thrown into. I didn't want to blacken my soul by abusing and eventually butchering innocents.

Seojun's eyes softened, and the warm smile he had given me when we were kids spread across his face. "You may be younger than everyone here, but you are wiser. You are right; this lifestyle makes me do things I am not proud of, but I'd be lying if I said I didn't enjoy my job. Shit, I downright love it. I am no fool, though; I know it's not meant for everybody.

My shoulders relaxed as I exhaled the breath I was holding.

"Akeno, you have a gentle soul, and God has placed you on another path. I am already a lost soul."

"That's the great thing about God; he's always waiting with open arms for you to return."

Seojun snorted as he stood up from his seat. "Nah, I'm far too gone, but who knows, maybe one day I'll change my life. If no one else tells you, I am proud of you – you'll be a great man when you get older."

I smiled and held out my hand for a handshake, as my mother and uncle had taught us. Hugs were too affectionate and frowned upon in my family. My cousin gripped my hand and gently tapped me on the shoulder.

"If you ever need my help, just say the word."

"Thanks, Seojun; I'll remember that when your aunt is ready to fight."

A frown formed on his lips. "She's still doing that, huh?"

I gave him a tight-lipped grin and nodded. He sighed and squeezed my shoulder before clapping me on the back. Seojun was the only person who knew how abusive my mother could be. Hell, his father was the same way with him.

We were two innocent kids once upon a time, but our parents cared more about power and money. They didn't care who they hurt in the process.

"Alright, get out of here, kid, and go have some fun."

I chuckled and dashed out of the door. It was just past 8 p.m., and I could be back on my side of town in thirty minutes. I didn't live too far from Luther, and I remembered he mentioned that Denice lived close by him. I shot him a quick message to drop their location when they made it to her house, and I was on my way.

"Akeno!"

I spun around, and I felt the wind rush out of me.

"C'mon, son, get in the car. We have to talk."

I stared at my dad with aggravation. I didn't want to go home, but by the anxious look on his face, I didn't have much of a choice.

Chapter 9

Denice

We had been at my house for barely forty-five minutes, and I was already over the night. I wanted to go to my room and finish reading my book rather than sit here. I mean, I only invited everyone to come over because 'everyone' included Ayzo, but he's not here. Therefore, I was not interested in sitting in the living room watching Luther, Xavier, and Olivia, passing around three blunts and getting high.

"I told you I had some good shit," Xavier coughed.

Olivia chuckled before inhaling the blunt and releasing smoke from her nose. "I can admit that I was wrong; my bad, X." She leaned back against the couch and closed her eyes. She squinted one eye open at me before smiling. "This is definitely worth keeping my mouth shut and not busting Denice's ass with her folks for having yall over."

"Aww, you were going to snitch on poor Denice?" Luther teased.

"Sure was, but I highly doubt her parents would've believed me. After all, Denice is just a perfect little angel. Prude, but innocent."

I rolled my eyes as they all began to laugh. Luther picked up the bottle of gin he had taken out of the convenience store I met Ayzo at earlier. I didn't think the cashier would allow him to just walk out with liquor, but he did. I couldn't help but wonder what that was all about, but then again, it didn't matter. Luther's red flags were soaring higher and higher and it was becoming easier to make the decision to stay away from him.

I watched as he poured himself a third cup. He added a splash of minute maid juice, but Olivia grabbed the cup out of his hands before he could take a sip. He watched her with hooded eyes as she teased the cup with her pink-coated lips before taking a sip.

"Oh shit." Xavier slurred before grabbing the bottle and making another drink himself.

Luther flicked his tongue across his bottom lip, practically eye fucking Olivia. Her ass knew what the fuck she was doing because she never drank after anybody. Hell, she hated smoking with other people half the time because of hygiene.

I stood up from the recliner and stomped toward the kitchen. I knew Luther was a womanizer, but the fact that he openly flirted and played in my face was beyond crazy. Of course, Olivia's ass was eating the shit up because she assumed it would bother me. Unfortunately for the both of them, I didn't give a rat's ass.

Luther and I were not together, and the only thing I allowed him to do was kiss me on my neck. That's it. I had no emotional ties towards him, and I for damn sure didn't care about Olivia. Her ass had one foot out the door anyway.

I exhaled through my nostrils and closed my eyes, allowing my head to fall back. I needed to get their ass out of here or find a way to go to my room undisturbed. Hell, who was I kidding? They probably wouldn't even notice if I were to leave.

A loud buzzing sound had me snapping my eyes open and peeking down at the kitchen counter. Luther had left his phone, and a text message had rolled in. I didn't want to pry—okay, let me not get the lying—I was about to be nosy as hell.

I swiped up his phone and typed in his passcode. I watched him type it in when he thought I wasn't paying attention. Hell, it was 1234; anybody could've guessed it. My tummy began to knot as I caught Ayzo's name appearing on the screen.

> I'm heading to that side of town. What's Denice's address so I can meet you all there?

I couldn't help the smile forming on my lips. When I saw Ayzo leave the car in the middle of nowhere, I was sure he would be too busy to hang out tonight. I damn near told Luther and Xavier to go away, but I didn't want to seem obvious. Ayzo was fine as hell, and there was an attraction between us the minute our hands touched at the store. I had no idea who he was, but I wanted to.

I stretched my fingers before swiftly typing out my address and sending it. I exhaled as I sat the phone down and grabbed a bottle of water. As much as I desired to hold on to Luther's phone just in case he texted back, I didn't need him to know that I learned his passcode and was in his texts.

Feeling excited again about the night, I returned to the living room. I halted in my steps when my eyes landed on the trio. Olivia was sandwiched between Xavier and Luther, her eyes closed and mouth slightly open. She rubbed the back of each boy's head as they sucked and licked both sides of her neck. Xavier had one hand on her breast as Luther had his cupping her sex.

I spun around and returned to the kitchen before they noticed I was there. Oh, hell no! I was not about to sit around here while Olivia got tossed up in the living room. They needed to get out of here with that mess. I exaggeratedly cleared my throat and coughed near the doorway to signal I was nearby. I could hear them shuffling around, so I waited a few moments before walking back into the room.

"So, what do y'all want to do now?" I asked indifferently.

"Uh, we gotta go make a stop by X's place and the store – we're out of supplies for another blunt," Luther said, standing up from the couch.

"I'm coming – I want to grab some snacks," Olivia said abruptly.

I wanted to laugh at the blatant lie, but I just nodded. "That's cool. I'm going to hang out here."

"Bet. We'll be back."

Luther, Olivia, and Xavier all filed out of the house one by one. I rolled my eyes and slumped back on the lazy boy recliner. Irritation attempted to creep up my spine until I remembered that Ayzo was on the way. A slight flutter swam through my core.

Chapter 10

Ayzo

My dad and I sat silently as we stared at our house from the driveway. Neither of us attempted to get out of the car, fearful of the havoc waiting for us. I felt my phone buzz in my pocket, reminding me that I had a text message waiting, but that was the least of my worries.

My dad picked me up and dropped a major bombshell, which was turning my life upside down. My mom and dad had been fooling around on each other right under my nose. Granted, they slept in two separate bedrooms, but I assumed my dad still loved my mom and wanted to give her space. Apparently, my good ole mother had been cheating on him for at least a year. When my dad initially found out, he was hurt and pissed off.

So, to get even with her infidelity and abuse, he decided to sleep with my mom's best friend, Mia. However, instead of being a one-time revenge ploy, they fell in love. During the car ride, my dad explained that he and Mia had come clean to Mom a few hours ago. They announced that they intended to move in together and that my dad was going to file for divorce.

I wouldn't say I liked that my parents were deliberately sleeping with other people outside of their marriage. Still, I couldn't help but feel the overwhelming relief that they were separating. I was elated that my dad found someone who loved and respected him. I've known Mia my whole life; she was always sweet and gentle. Honestly, I wasn't even sure how she was friends with my mom.

My dad let out a hefty sigh. "I know this all came out unexpectedly, but you are old enough to understand that your dad is tired. I'm tired of not being brave enough to keep you safe and allowing your mom to treat us the way she has for so long."

"Dad," I began, but he clutched my shoulder and pivoted me toward him.

"Akeno, I apologize for not stepping in and keeping you safe. I should have taken every hit that she gave to you."

"How could you? You were just as bruised and beaten as me. I don't blame you or hold anything against you. I want you to be happy."

He beamed and drew me in for a quick hug. "Alright, so what's going to be your choice? Do you want to stay here and finish the school year with your mom? Or move with me but start over at a new school?"

No brainer, right? It would make sense for me to move with my dad, where I'd be protected and have a chance of a normal life. How could I just up and move from the life I was used to, though? Outside of dealing with my mom, I loved it here—all the friends I made and the new ones I wanted to get to know. Denice flashed through my mind.

Smash!

My train of thought was interrupted by the sound of loud cracking echoing throughout the car. My dad and I shrank in our seats as the front windshield of his car fractured.

"What the fuck, Kim!" my dad shouted as he jumped out of the car.

My mom was standing on the hood of the car with a bat in her hand. She jumped down and charged for my dad. He tried to reach for her, but she was quick. She drew her arm back and punched him in the nose while driving the bat into his groin.

"Fuck!" he groaned, dropping to the ground.

"Dad!" I shouted as I watched in horror.

My mother cackled as she jumped back on the hood and glared at me. Her brown eyes were protruding and manic as she raised the bat over her head. I jumped out of the car and knelt beside my dad, watching as she brought it down on the windshield again.

Whack!

An ear-splitting crash echoed, followed by my dad's gasp.

"Think you can just fuck me over?" she yelled, jumping off the hood of the car. She threw down the bat again, shattering the rearview window. "Wait until I get my hands on Mia!"

"Mom, stop!" I ran up to her and tried to snatch the bat from her. She backhanded me, her ring slicing into my lip. The tangy taste of copper filled my mouth as I stumbled back.

"Fuck away from me, you little shit."

"Real nice mom! How are you going to be upset with dad for finding love when you clearly hate us? Besides, you were cheating first!"

Smack!

My head flew to the side as she punched me across the face. Heat coursed through my body, and I wanted nothing more than to show my mother how lethal I was, but I didn't. At the end of the day she was still my mom, no matter how screwed up she was.

I held up my hands and took several steps back towards my dad.

"You have done nothing but hold me back! I should have left you with the Jaguars the minute I gave birth so you could grow into a real man! And you," my mom spat, pointing the bat at my dad. "I regret the day I opened my legs for your pathetic ass. I should have listened to my brother and had you beaten for getting me pregnant, but noooo! My stupid heart had me thinking that I actually loved your weak ass."

She swung the bat one final time, knocking out the side mirrors before tossing it to the ground. She spat at our feet before stomping up the driveway, grabbing her duffle bag, and hopping in her car. She began backing out, but I realized she wasn't aiming for the street.

The back tires ran off the pavement and through the grass straight for us. I pushed my dad out of the way and leaped to the opposite side. A loud screeching noise echoed as she spun onto the street, barely missing my legs.

"Good riddance!" she screamed, throwing us the middle finger before taking off.

My heart pounded against my chest. Knowing my mother, she was on her way to see Uncle Chul-Moo. He was her only sibling, and he practically raised her. In other words, my uncle would do anything for my mother whenever she was upset. Everyone knew it was wise not to push her to the point where she got her brother involved. Hell, when I was twelve, my mom had one of the nail technicians shot to death for causing her to bleed when she was getting her cuticles cut.

"We leave in the morning," I said, helping my dad off the ground. My chest heaved with fury as I stared at the red brake lights in the distance. My dad and I gave each other knowing looks before rushing into the house and packing as much of our belongings as possible.

"Mia, baby," my dad said frantically on the phone. "Get to my house as soon as you can. I don't care about all of your stuff. I packed a few duffle bags in your trunk before I left – get in the car and get over here now."

I knew that my mom didn't particularly like me or my dad, and I knew she was on her way to have us beaten or, as mad as she was, killed. Mia would be the first to go.

I quickly grabbed my phone and texted Seojun, the one person who could help or give us time to leave the city.

"I need a favor."

Chapter 11

Denice

As the recurring flashback played through my dreams, I tossed and turned in my sleep. Screams, puddles of blood, and black body bags swam through my mind over and over again – like an instant replay every time I closed my eyes.

I clutched at my throat due to the stinging sensation from all of the yelling I did when my dad had my mother's hair fisted in his hand while he held the blade of his pocket knife against her throat.

"I love you two so much," he cried, rubbing his forehead against my mom's temple. "I won't let anyone take you away from me."

"Daddy, please! Let mommy go!"

"Denice, baby, your mommy was trying to leave. She was going to leave and take you away from me - take away her love from me!"

My mom grunted as angry tears fell down her eyes. "Rico, you are out of control. You got me fired from work for constantly calling the office line when I didn't respond to you fast enough. You go through my phone to make sure I'm not cheating. Hell, you almost ran down our neighbor for helping me with the garbage when you were passed out drunk."

"You were fucking that nigga! I've seen how he's looked at you," my dad snarled, gripping her hair tighter.

"Fuck you, Rico - you're fucking crazy!"

"Daddy, please just let her go," I whimpered.

"Baby girl, don't you see what she's doing to us? She's trying to tear our family apart. I love you both so much, and I need y'all."

I watched as tears pooled in his eyes. I knew my mom loved my dad, but she expressed to him that she felt suffocated. He was constantly watching and following her every move – continually drinking and assuming that she was cheating. He snapped when my mom finally told my dad she couldn't take it anymore.

"Denice, run, baby! Get out of here!" my mom shouted as she threw her head back, smashing it against my dad's nose.

"Fuck!" he groaned.

My mom sprinted toward me, but she wasn't fast enough. My dad had captured her by the back of her collar and threw her down, her head smacking against the ground with an echoing thud. He threw his body on top of her and jammed the knife into her side. My mom let out a piercing scream that made my heart drop.

"If I can't have you or my family, then nobody will!"

With that, he tore the knife out of her and plunged it into her chest. I watched as my dad picked up my mother's head and planted kisses across her face as tears of pain streaked her cheeks. She coughed up blood but continued to slap and push against him. He murmured how much he loved her and promised that me and him would be right behind her.

I was frozen in fear, and everything seemed to be moving in slow motion. My mother's hand gripped my dad's shirt but slowly released it, letting her hand fall to the ground. She let out a soft whimper as she looked over at me before she exhaled her final breath. She was gone.

My dad crushed his lips against hers and mumbled how much he loved her. I couldn't breathe. I couldn't move. One minute, my mom and I were apartment shopping and planning our escape, and now, she was gone. Suddenly, my dad snapped his head toward me while pulling the knife out of my mom.

"C'mon, baby. You, Mommy, and I are going to a new place. We're all going to be together forever. This is what people who love each other do—make sure they and their families are together forever."

I shook my head.

"Why are you afraid? You and I are so much alike, so this shouldn't be new for you."

"No!" I cried, fear and bile inching up my throat as my dad began strolling closer to me. "I am not like you!"

A manic laugh bubbled out of his mouth as he scratched the tip of the knife against his temple. "Oh, Denice, baby girl – you are more like me than you know. We love the same and fight to protect what's ours."

My hands trembled as his words raced through my mind. I realized that he was right – I was just like him. Throughout the years, countless people told me how much I resembled and acted like my dad. They used to joke that my mom had nothing to do with giving birth to me because I was an exact replica of him.

I was only eight, but I loved hard, and I was constantly in trouble for fighting for my friends or those I loved when they were getting picked on. My dad loved and fought for the people he loved, too. Tears streaked my face as I shook my head. I guess I was going to turn out just like him – loving and violent.

Suddenly, he sprinted full speed toward me, causing me to scream. I turned on my heels and bolted out the door. I moved my little legs down the stairs as fast as I could while tears blurred my vision. I opened the bathroom door and slammed it shut to make him think I was hiding there. I always hid in the bathroom when I was scared or in trouble and figured that'd be the first place he'd look. I quietly snuck out the back door and crawled underneath the porch as I held my breath.

"Denice! Dammit, girl, where the hell are you?"

I could hear my dad calling for me inside the house as I clamped my eyes shut and prayed that he wouldn't find me.

After a few moments, a loud bang echoed throughout the house, causing me to scream. Then everything was quiet.

I jolted out of my sleep and tried to catch my breath. Beads of sweat trickled across my forehead, and my tank top stuck to my skin. I reached over and grabbed my phone off the side table. It was just after 11 pm – I had fallen asleep, and my heart was racing from the nightmare.

I stood up from the couch and stretched. It wasn't the first time I'd had that nightmare. I've dreamt about that day more than I liked. When I was younger, I used to scream and cry, causing Mama Julia and Dad Erin to stay in my room until I was able to sleep again. They wanted me to see a therapist, but I didn't see a point in it.

My dad loved my mom so much that he would have rather killed the entire family than let us go. Talking to some stranger wasn't going to bring my mom back. It wasn't going to erase the memory of my mom's scared look as the knife protruded from her chest.

I walked to the bathroom, shaking my head as I turned the shower on. I didn't need to see a therapist. I knew the life lesson – don't fall in love. Love made people do stupid, irrational things. Love was jealous, chaotic, dangerous, unpredictable, and deadly. As long as I stayed away from it, I would be fine. As long as I kept people away from me and ensured they didn't love me, I wouldn't turn out like my dad.

I stepped into the shower, letting the scorching water cascade over me. I lathered my body with my vanilla-scented exfoliating scrub and tried to erase the memory. After I was satisfied, I turned off the shower and wrapped my body in a towel. I strolled to my bedroom and grabbed my pink pajama shorts and white tank top.

As soon as I unpinned my hair, letting it fall into a damp, wild, curly afro, I heard a knock at the door. I scrunched up my nose as I pulled on my socks and headed toward the front. Olivia ass must've forgotten her damn key.

I unlocked and pulled the door open, not bothering to look through the peephole. I stood frozen in when I was met by a pair of light brown eyes. A slight grin lifted at one side of Ayzo's lips as he looked me up and down. Crap, how could I have forgotten that he was coming? I was literally waiting up for him until my dumbass fell asleep and had that nightmare. Now, here I was, all discombobulated.

"Hey, Dee."

"Ayzo," I beamed, staring at him.

He changed from his simple tank top and basketball shorts to a pair of black jeans with designer rips around the knees and a white T-shirt. His hair was pulled up into a bun, and a silver necklace with a cross at the end hung from his neck, matched by a pair of small silver loop earrings. The sweet smell of mint, lavender, and cedarwood filled my nose, and I swear my mouth was about to start watering.

He licked his lips, and I couldn't help but notice the tiny cut. What happened to him? Did he get into a fight?

"So, can I come in?"

Hell no, don't do it, Denice! I shouted in my mind. I couldn't trust what I'd do if I let him in this house with no one else around. He was so damn sexy, and he wasn't even trying.

Okay, get it together, Denice. I've been around plenty of cute boys before and didn't do anything stupid – I got this.

I stepped aside, "come in."

Chapter 12
Ayzo

I never thought some plain pink pajama shorts would be one of my turn-ons. When my eyes landed on Denice in her simple sleepwear with her damp natural hair freely falling past her shoulders, I wanted to grab her by the back of her neck and kiss her until her knees gave out.

It's crazy how one simple look at Denice made me forget everything that's happened in the past few hours, and I had absolutely no problem with that. I came over with the intent to spend time with my friends one last time before I traveled to the East

Coast, but at this point, I couldn't have cared less about them. Denice had my complete attention.

"Where's everybody?" I asked, stepping inside and sitting on the couch.

"They said they were going to pick up more supplies to smoke."

I bobbed my head. "Wonder why Luther didn't mention that in the text earlier. I could've met them at the store."

She nervously shifted her weight from one foot to the other as she stood by the front entry. She chewed on her bottom lip before running her hand through her curls. "He, uh, he didn't know that you were coming."

I cocked my head to the side with an arched eyebrow. She let out a breath of air before walking over to sit next to me on the couch.

"Well, I was the one who texted you my address from Luther's phone. I wanted you to come over, and when I saw your message, I just went for it. Plus, at the moment, Luther was, uh, preoccupied, so I texted for him."

"Is that right? So, it's just me and you here?"

She nodded. "Hope that's okay. You and I know that as soon as you've come over, Luther would have been all in my face - just like a child seeking attention."

"That part."

"Right! Besides, how would I have gotten to know you better if he was going to be bothering me?"

A smile quirked at the corner of my mouth as I inched closer to her on the couch. She blushed with a nervous chuckle before crossing one leg over the other. My heart raged with excitement for the simple act.

As I mentioned, when I was heading over here, my mind was nowhere near anything sexual. Hell, it was the last thing on my mind. I wanted to enjoy the company of good friends, maybe try weed for the first time, and have a few drinks to numb out the past few hours.

Now that I was alone with Denice, my thinking was becoming chaotic. Everything my grandfather and dad drilled into my brain about waiting for marriage to be intimate with someone was getting Jazzy Jeffed – thrown out the door.

"You know, I was lowkey pissed that you hopped out of the car earlier. I didn't want to hang out with only Luther and Xavier."

"I thought you and Luther were a thing, though."

She shook her head. "I had a small crush, and we dated for less than seventy-two hours. The idea of us rekindling anything was thrown out the window when I walked in on him and Xavier about to have an entire threesome with my foster sister."

I gaped at her in disbelief, with my mouth hung open. "For real?"

She nodded, "wandered in and witnessed them right here on the couch. I shouldn't be surprised, though. I knew Luther was a hoe, but I just got caught up in his bullshit lies."

"Damn, I'm sorry, Dee."

"Why? We weren't dating or anything of the sort. He is more than welcome to date or fuck whomever he pleases. Besides, I was glad he went after her instead of me. I for damn sure didn't want him to touch me or try to get in my panties. Plus, I could be with you, unbothered."

We gazed at each other, tension filling the room before I cleared my throat. "Welp, since it's going to be me and you for a bit, what do you want to do?"

She wetted her lips, causing my body to tingle all over. "How about we watch a movie? Have you seen Insidious? It's pretty scary but good."

"I'm not a huge scary movie fan."

"I'll protect you," she said, standing up and extending her hand.

I laughed quietly and captured her hand, enjoying her warm touch. She was not only fine but bold. Most girls played that 'I'm too shy' card, not Denice. She was taking control, and I was all for it.

My stomach did somersaults as she pulled me to her bedroom, and I couldn't help but enjoy my view. With each bounce of her round cheeks, as we swiftly moved through the hall, my pants became tighter and tighter. Shit, I needed to get myself together. I didn't want her to turn around and get an eye full of my perverted ass, but I couldn't help myself.

I sat on her bed as she flipped through Netflix to find the movie. For a brief moment, I thought about leaving. Why was I getting close to her if there was no chance I'd see her again? Maybe I should stay with my mom so I can have more time with Denice.

Fuck that, I was definitely leaving, but I didn't want to abandon Denice. I let out a small breath. I was going to make the best out of this night with her. We will watch the movie, maybe chat a bit more, and then I will be gone. No harm, no foul.

She settled in next to me as the movie played when her phone began to vibrate on the nightstand. She hesitated before reaching over and snatching it up. She briefly skimmed through the notification before smacking her lips and tossing it back on the table.

"Everything okay?"

"Yeah, just Luther asking if I wanted to hang out at Xavier's place. I'll pass. Besides, I'm with the one I want to hang out with."

I could feel my face flush as she gave me a quick wink before returning to the movie. I kept my face neutral, but on the inside, I was grinning extra hard. Denice had my ass feeling all giddy and shit. Corny? Yeah, I know, that's how good she had me feeling.

We had only been watching the movie for about thirty minutes, and she wasn't lying. The film was scary as hell, and as much as I tried to play hard, my ass was terrified.

"Oh fuck!" I yelped as I grabbed her thigh without realizing it. This red demon suddenly popped up on the screen, causing me to jump out of my skin.

"Shit!" she chuckled. "I forgot about that damn part. Are you okay?" She asked, pausing the movie.

I cleared my throat. "Y-yeah."

I really wasn't, and from the look she was giving me, she knew my soul momentarily left my body from fright.

She comfortably rubbed my arm, "Told you, scary, but good."

"Hell yeah, but I'd be totally okay if we didn't finish the movie and put on some cartoons."

She snorted out a laugh. "We can do that, but only if it's The Powerpuff Girls."

"Oh wow! You just going to ignore my homie Courage the Cowardly Dog?"

"Oh, absolutely! That show is just as scary as a horror film."

We laughed some more, and I couldn't help but notice that she hadn't stopped rubbing my arm. I kept my hand on her leg and idly stroked my thumb across her thigh. Our laughter began to die, and soon, the only noise around was the continued vibrating of Denice's phone with text message notifications. Denice let out a loud, annoyed sigh but made no attempt to reach for her phone.

Damn, Luther's ass was tripping if he was blowing up her phone like that. I mean, he was just dicking down her foster sister. You'd think his ass would need a break before trying to find someone else to fuck. Then again, I noticed how territorial he was regarding Denice, but it was easy to see why.

I sat my back against the wall and peeked over at Denice. She glanced at her phone and then back at me before resting her head on my shoulder. She tensed, waiting for my reaction, but when I rubbed her back, she relaxed further into me. Being around her felt, I don't know - right. All of my problems and stress melted away the minute I laid eyes on her, and the longer I was in her presence, the more at ease I was. It felt like I'd known her my entire life - as if she was meant just for me, even though we barely knew each other. I hated that I could only be with her for merely one night.

Denice exhaled a shuttering breath before slowly looking up at me. I froze and stared back at her as she bit onto her bottom lip. I wondered what was going on in her head. Was she feeling the same thing I was, or was I allowing my cluttered thoughts to go crazy?

She huffed out a nervous giggle before she laid her head back on my shoulder. Resting her hand on my knee, she slowly dragged it up my inner thigh before moving it back to my knee. Denice repeated this motion a few times as she flicked her tongue across her lips. I could feel my dick waking up with excitement. We were playing a dangerous game, but I wasn't about to stop her.

Before I knew it, she lifted her head off me and climbed onto my lap. I immediately placed my hands around her hips like it was second nature. She inched down and pressed her forehead against mine.

"Akeno, I have never done anything like this before, but something about you is drawing me towards you and telling me to keep you close."

I closed my eyes and gripped her hips tighter, letting out a low growl as she slowly rocked into me. What the hell was she doing to me? How could this girl I'd barely known have me in such a chokehold right now?

Dammit, I need to go! I can't do this to her. As much as I wanted to taste her lips and get to know her intimately, I couldn't. I never wanted to be the type of person to fuck and then disappear — only fuck niggas did that shit. Besides, Denice deserved so much more.

I opened my eyes and stared back into the affectionate ones, pinning me with a lustful, wanting gaze. I arched an eyebrow as I reconsidered the situation. Maybe Denice would understand. If I told her the truth about everything happening to me, perhaps we could stay close. I mean, I'd be thousands of miles away, but I think she'd understand.

Why couldn't I have fun for once? I mean, I just wanted one night. I wanted to indulge in entertainment and not have to worry whether or not I was going to be beaten because my mom was pissed off. Not having to worry about completing deadly jobs by being the shadow and not having to worry about school. I licked my lips and swallowed.

"Then keep me close," I whispered before smashing my lips against hers.

We ignored her phone as Luther's name flashed across the screen again.

Chapter 13

Ayzo

Denice and I wanted each other, but I didn't want to take her innocence. Not because I didn't want to experience my first time with her but because I couldn't stay in Chicago. I wanted a chance to start over and have an everyday teenage life, and I couldn't do that if I lingered. Besides, I'd feel like a complete asshole if we took it to the point of no return, and I just left.

I examined Denice's sleeping face and traced my fingers across her lips. I wanted to memorize every inch of her because I knew I wouldn't have the chance to see her again. Well, no time soon anyway. What we shared was beautiful. Her touch, her lips, everything about her felt amazing. Hell, I wanted more of her. I wanted to take things to that next step and was on the verge of waking Dee up with a changed mind, but I didn't.

I dropped my hand and sighed. Guilt began creeping up my spine. The disappointed look on Denice's face when I told her we couldn't have sex made my insides churn. I had rejected her with false promises that we could try again when we were older. She had no clue I wasn't staying around to make her mine.

Ugh! She was going to hate me. I should have fucking left as soon as she sat on my lap. I usually had no problem with controlling my urges and never allowed myself to go past light touching. What the fuck was I thinking? Yeah, I wanted to have fun, but now I felt like shit.

I rubbed my hand down my face and glanced at the clock on her nightstand. It was just after three in the morning, and we were leaving for Philly in a few hours. I slowly got out of the bed and threw my clothes back on. I grabbed a piece of paper off her desk and wrote her a quick note with my phone number. I prayed that she wouldn't be too pissed and give me a call.

Leaving Denice a swift kiss on her forehead, I ran my hands down the side of her face one more time. I wish I had met her sooner – then we'd run away together. I shook my head before stepping over to open the window. Thankful that she was in a one-story house, I glanced at her again before jumping out.

"I see everybody was getting some pussy tonight."

I spun around to see Luther taking a drag from his cigarette, leaning against his car. He looked between me and the window before flicking it to the ground.

"Yo, Luther –"

"You know, I thought we were cool Ayzo. How are you gonna stick your dick in my property?"

"Huh? What the fuck are you talking about?"

"I told you Denice was mine, but here you are sneaking out of her window like the backstabbing bitch that you are."

"First of all, Denice is a person, not your damn property – have some fucking respect on her name. Second of all, what me and Dee were doing has nothing to do with you. I am not about to talk about our business. Third, I heard you and X were having fun with her foster sister. So, I suggest you worry about yourself and never call me out of my muthafuckin name."

"So what if we were tossing up her easy-ass sister? She was just a piece of ass paying for her share of the weed she wanted to partake in. Denice belongs to me! If I find out that you touched what belongs to me, I'll fucking kill you."

"Nigga you fucking tripping," I spat, twisting to walk away.

I heard him move away from the car and trail behind me. Luther had no idea what I was capable of since I used to be the shadow, and I wanted nothing more than to show him, but I didn't. Instead, I allowed him to grab my arm and turn me around to face him.

"Don't turn your back on me!"

"Y'all chill!" Xavier yelled in a low voice as he slowly closed the front door, held onto his pants, and jogged towards us. "I can hear you two muthafuckas from the living room."

He buckled his pants and shook his head as he mumbled that we almost fucked up his nut from all our yelling. I rolled my eyes as Luther threw his arm over his shoulder.

"You see, Ayzo, X is a good friend. He knew that Denice was off limits, and because of that, I allowed him to share her hoe-ass sister with me. Shit, he just got seconds. If you want to roll with me and have my protection in these streets, then you need to remember that I get first dibs."

The fuck? His ass couldn't be serious. I looked over at Xavier, who only stared down at the ground. This fool was really cool with Luther's twisted version of prima nocta and willingly hung out with him.

"Fuck you," I expressed, pointing at Luther. Then I pointed at Xavier, "You're delusional if you think this muthafucka is your friend."

With that, I spun on my heels and strode off. As I mentioned before, Luther was my oldest friend, but his ass was talking recklessly, and I'd be damned if I wanted that type of friendship.

He had been slowly changing into someone I didn't recognize. It sucked that I was losing a old friend, but everything must come to an end – including friendships. Who knows, maybe I'd find a better friend in Philly.

Chapter 14

Denice

I rolled over and reached for Ayzo, but the rest of my bed was empty. A shot of alarm surged through my body until I heard the toilet flush from my private bathroom, and I relaxed. I ran my hand down my face and laughed at myself. Jeez, this boy had me giddy and anxious for him after just one night and we didn't even have sex.

"You're already getting attached? Just like your dad," my intrusive thoughts yelled.

No! I shook my head, ignoring that quiet voice. I wasn't like my dad – I was my own person. I took a shuddering breath and counted backwards until my breathing evened again. I had a great time with Ayzo last night and I wasn't about to ruin it with negativity.

Massaging my eyes, I grudgingly snatched my phone off the nightstand and saw it was five in the morning. I was usually a morning person, but not this damn early. Then I realized I had twenty missed calls and fifteen text notifications – all from Luther. What the hell? I let out a groan and tossed my phone down on the bed. I didn't have the energy to deal with his ass yet.

I yawned and stood up from the bed for a much-needed stretch. I walked over to the bathroom and lifted my hand to knock when the door swung open. My smile withered as Olivia stood before me.

"Well, well, look who's finally awake."

"What the hell are you doing in my room? Where is Akeno?"

"What the hell is an Akeno?"

I rolled my eyes and shook my head. I realized that he was already gone before she came into my room. Why would he leave without telling me, though? Maybe he had gotten scared and left if he heard my parents. Oh crap, what about his parents? They were probably pissed that he was gone all night.

Olivia gathered her hair and tossed it into a messy bun before giving me a sly smirk. "Has Luther texted you yet?"

I frowned, "Shouldn't you be asking yourself that?"

She wiped at the corners of her mouth and dragged her bottom lip between her teeth as her eyes glazed over. Her smile widened before she cocked her head to the side. "I have no idea what you are talking about."

"Sure you don't. Now get the hell out of my room."

"Ah, I am going to miss your unattractive looks and attitude. Wait, who am I kidding? No, I won't. Besides, you're just jealous that Luther wanted me, not you."

"Oh yeah," I exaggerated. "I sure am jealous of being tossed up like a cheap hoe by a man whore and his clingy friend."

She snarled before bumping past me and knocking all the papers off my desk before storming out of my room. Good riddance.

****

I sat on the park bench with an iced coffee and a copy of Mary B Morrison's If I Can't Have You. It was just after seven, and the cool morning air and stillness seemed evident, so I enjoyed the outdoors before the city woke up. My adoptive parents asked if I wanted to join them in taking Olivia to meet her mom, but I declined. I said my final farewells to her ass, and I desired to protect my energy.

"I thought I would find you here."

I shot my head up to see Luther strolling toward me. I quietly groaned as I placed my bookmark back into my book and sat it down. Luther was a morning person like me. Hell, that's how we even started talking.

I looked around, hoping to see Ayzo, but was saddened to learn he was alone. My mind wandered off to Ayzo. Was he a morning person, too? It would have been nice to have enjoyed this time with him, but I had no way of contacting him. I could ask Luther, but that would do nothing but cause unwanted problems.

"Good morning, Luther."

"Ew, why did you say it all dry? Like you weren't happy to see me?" Luther questioned as he took out his Stephen King's Doctor Sleep copy.

As much as Luther irritated me and tried to act like he was this hard street guy, he was a total book nerd like me. Before the sun fully rose or everyone else was awake, Luther and I would sit outside enjoying the silence and escaping in our books.

It was one of the things I liked about him, and at first, I thought it was enough to like him as a boyfriend. However, I saw how he acted when we were no longer alone. The minute the city woke up, Luther's ugly side did, too.

"I'm actually not all that happy to see you. Why were you blowing up my phone like that?"

"You weren't answering me!"

"And? Besides, I thought you, Xavier, and Olivia were entertaining each other," I stated sarcastically.

Luther scoffed, "You're one to talk."

"What the fuck does that mean?"

Before I knew it, Luther grabbed me by the arm and hauled me onto my feet. His grip tightened, and I struggled to break his hold. No matter how much I tugged, he didn't budge.

"Did you let that nigga fuck?"

"W-what?"

Luther bared his teeth as he yanked me closer, his nose brushing mine. "You heard me. Did you let Ayzo fuck? I saw him sneaking out of your window at three this morning. What the fuck were y'all doing?"

My head spun as I tried to digest his words. Ayzo snuck out of my room at three? I didn't remember exactly what time I fell asleep, but I remembered seeing the time on my phone reading 2:30 am. So, he waited thirty minutes before tiptoeing out? But why? We had a great time together - I thought he liked me.

My stomach began to churn with the realization that I had been used. I was suddenly thankful that Ayzo turned me down for sex because I would feel ten times worse right about now. Ugh! I knew I should have kept to myself this summer. I shouldn't have involved myself with any of these guys. All I knew right now was the fact that I was done with these muthafuckas. I knew I should have kept my distance, but now I was heartbroken and felt like an idiot.

"Fuck off me, Luther," I shouted, pushing him with all of the strength that I could muster up, causing him to stumble back. "And for your information, no, we didn't have sex."

"Good! You belong to me, Denice. Nobody touches or gets to have you first except for me," Luther barked between gritted teeth.

My mouth hung open. "Excuse me?"

Luther lowered his head to meet me eye to eye. "Your virginity belongs to me. You are my property."

"You're fucking crazy!"

"I'll be that for you because you are mine!"

Anger and fear coursed through my body. The crazed look dancing in his eyes reminded me of how my dad looked when he attacked my mother. No! I wasn't going to end up like her. My flight or fight instincts were kicking in, and I wouldn't be frozen in fear this time.

I reared my arm back and punched him. Luther fell on his ass, blood streaming from his nose as he yelled out in pain. My hand trembled, but the adrenaline pumping through me made me feel numb.

"You've lost your fucking mind. All of you can stay away from me!" I cried.

With that, I collected my book and ran back to my house.

I never spoke to Luther after that, and Ayzo disappeared. I felt a mixture of being manipulated and afraid. Luther and I didn't do anything sexually, and yet he had some claim over me that made him act crazy. While Ayzo and I fooled around, he vanished, causing me to feel pure hatred for him.

When school started back up, I thought things would be better. At first, I made a few friends, but fear took over. What if they began to act like Luther, too? What if I started to like another guy, but he just used me like Ayzo, and my deep hatred caused me to have thoughts of hurting them?

I didn't want to risk it, so I instantly became an outsider. I was liked and cordial enough to be invited to parties and have a group of friends. Hell, there were even guys who wanted to date me, but I kept them all at a distance. I was too afraid of allowing anyone else to get close to me, and I vowed that I would not end up like my mother. Or worse, like my father.

I still saw Luther from time to time. He was still chasing after every girl in my school as well as some of the older women in the neighborhood. I tried my best to avoid him, but it seemed as if we always ended up at the same places. The grocery store, the park, in the school parking lot. Everywhere I was, his dark eyes bore holes in my back. It stayed that way until I graduated and moved.

Part II
Present

Chapter 15

Denice

I stared at Ayzo as he opened and closed his mouth – everything he desired to tell me clinging from his lips. Ugh! Why won't he talk to me? Why doesn't he just tell me the fucking truth! If I was more than just a potential fuck, then it shouldn't be hard to communicate the events that occurred that night. I wanted to believe he wasn't the type to go ghost, but the evidence was stacked against him.

I smacked my lips as I rolled my eyes. I didn't have time for this bullshit. I downed the rest of my drink and bumped past him. I didn't care about what he had to say. The past needed to stay where it was – no need to reminisce on our brief time together. Besides, as I mentioned before, we were young and dumb. We made poor decisions, and then he faded into thin air. End of story. Just as I opened the door to walk back into the apartment, I heard Ayzo let out a frustrated breath.

"I couldn't agree more," I said, closing the door behind me.

The remainder of the evening was spent playing Uno, Dominos, and Monopoly. I was actually enjoying myself and allowing my competitive spirit to take over. After a few more drinks and landslide wins, my aggravation toward Ayzo was gone. It didn't mean we would be friends again, but at least I could be in the same room as him for a few hours as we played board games without wanting to punch him in the face.

"I need a snack from Denice's ass-kicking," Nick grumbled, getting up from his seat.

"Ditto," Ayzo laughed, following.

I smirked and did a little shimmy in my seat. I warned everyone that I was competitive. I didn't care what game I played; I aimed to win.

"So," Ashlynn said, getting up and sitting beside me. "Are you going to finally tell me how you and Ayzo know each other? It's been over six months now, and your 'I'll tell you later' excuse isn't going to work anymore. I'm patient but not that damn patient."

I peeked over my shoulder and saw the guys in the kitchen laughing, not paying us attention. I bit onto my bottom lip before circling back to my friend.

"Honestly, it's not much to tell. We met when I was sixteen and hung out this one time. That's it."

"Un-huh. So why do you have such animosity against him? I haven't known Ayzo long, but he seems like a decent man."

"Ugh," I groaned, leaning back against the couch. "Fine! He, uh, he gave me my first orgasm. We didn't have sex, but he has been the only man I've allowed to touch me intimately."

"What!" Ashlynn squealed out before I quickly covered her mouth.

"Please don't make a big scene, Lynn, and for goodness sake, don't repeat this to Nick. I'm pretty sure he and Akeno talk about everything."

She wrinkled her nose before bobbing her head in agreement to stay hushed. I double-checked the men were still preoccupied before slowly moving my hand from her mouth.

Ashlynn leaned closer to me before speaking. "Do you mean to tell me that you've never had sex? Not even once?"

I shook my head.

"But, you and Ayzo fooled around years ago?"

I nodded, downing the rest of my drink.

"It doesn't make sense – you've told me about some much kinky shit."

"You know I am a smutty dark romance book lover. Everything I told you was from things I've read and/or watched in porn videos that I wanted to eventually try. Plus, I didn't want to be judged."

"You know I would never judge you."

I smiled, "I know love. Besides, it's not like I didn't try it with Akeno. I gave myself to him, but he rejected me. Well, sort of. Like I said, we both climaxed together, but he didn't want to go all the way. He promised we'd try again when we were older. So, I assumed that he'd be around and we'd eventually start dating, but I was wrong. He snuck out of my house in the middle of the night and disappeared. I felt so used. So yeah, fuck Akeno."

"Damn, I'm sorry, Dee. I would've never pictured Ayzo doing no foul shit like that."

I nodded in agreement. I should have never sat on his damn lap that night. I shouldn't have allowed him into my bedroom.

"Well, what are you waiting for now?"

"You know it's weird, but I never felt a desire to have sex like when I was with Akeno. I said that when I made it to college, I was going to give it a try, but the days turned into weeks and then years, and here we are - a twenty-four-year-old virgin."

"Mmm, well, from what I've seen these past few months, Ayzo has been trying to get back on your good side. Maybe he was scared back then and wants to try again?"

"That's too bad. He's a day late and a dollar short. If he hadn't just left without uttering a word like a spineless coward, I may be inclined to entertain him, but nope. We had some mind-blowing foreplay, and then poof, he evaporated."

"Damn! What kind of foreplay were y'all doing to make this man chase after you after all these years?" Ashlynn chuckled.

"Lynn!" I playfully nudged her on the shoulder as we laughed out loud.

I wasn't about to admit to her that Ayzo had been filtering through my mind over the years, too. Shit, he wasn't the only one sprung off of one encounter. We may have been inexperienced before, but my body still reacted to our brief time together. Hell, the mere mention of him made me soaked.

Seeing his face and body mature into a grown man made it impossible not to imagine all of the new tricks he may have learned throughout the years. I know I've seen some things in videos that I wouldn't mind trying on him, but oh well. If he didn't want to be honest with me, I wouldn't give him a chance.

"Well," Ashlynn said chipperly, breaking me out of my thoughts. "Just wait until you find the man that you're in love with. Y'all won't be able to keep your hands off each other."

I scoffed. "No offense, Lynn, but fuck love. It's the ultimate intimate act that ties your soul to another individual, and for any person to say that they can fuck without getting attached is a liar. I've watched enough viral videos of people doing some crazy shit for getting attached to somebody."

"But love is so beautiful."

"Love and sex are the two deadliest combinations that can drive a person insane. Besides, it's just a dick. I have toys that can bring me to a toe-curling climax – no man required."

I watched Ashlynn's face turn into a frown before sympathy etched in her eyes. Dammit, I shouldn't have opened my mouth. She possibly couldn't understand where I was coming from. Lynn has always had a big heart and loves everything about love. So, of course, she'd be sad if someone rejected the idea of love.

I shook my head and sighed. I didn't want her to show me any pity. I was comfortable with my life. I didn't need love and sex to be happy. I had my own business, my books, and my closest friend in my life. I had money in my bank account, and I could travel when and wherever I wanted to – hell, what more could I ask for?

"Lynn, don't worry. I promise I am satisfied with my life," I said, drawing her into a hug. "I don't need sex, and I for damn sure do not need love. Well, not including spiritual love because you know I love you like you were my own sister. I meant that shit that could drive a person crazy if the wrong partner was chosen."

Ashlynn gave me a knowing look and squeezed my hand. She knew everything that happened to my mom and dad when I was younger. It took years, but I finally confided in her about that night our senior year in college. She never judged me or told anyone else, which made me love her even more as my best friend.

"All I'm going to say is that I don't think we were meant to walk this earth alone. If we have a chance to experience love with someone, we should take it instead of shoving it away. Some of the most beautiful Bible verses celebrate love. Take Ecclesiastes chapter four, verses nine through twelve."

"Hold on, let me open my Bible app. You know I don't know as many verses as you," I chuckled, retrieving my phone. I pinched my brows together as I finished reading the verses. "And what is this supposed to mean?"

"It means, just like I said – we were not meant to walk alone. How can you reject love but turn around and say that you love God?"

I swallowed the lump in my throat before sighing and tossing my phone back into my purse. Ashlynn gave me a smug look, and I wanted to smack it off. We both knew that she had a valid point. It's not like I didn't love amicably; I didn't see myself loving someone more than that. What if they loved like how my dad did? Even worse, what if I did? I didn't want to find out.

"Look, it's getting late. I'm going to head home." I finally spoke out.

"Fine," Ashlynn snorted before standing up. She knew she had gotten to me but was allowing me to sulk without rubbing it in my face. "Me and Nick will walk you to the car."

I nodded as she headed towards the kitchen, still snickering. Luckily, she was my sister because I would've thrown my shoe at her. I exhaled. I understand what the word says, but it didn't make it easier. I mean, I watched love destroy my family, and yet I'm supposed to have open arms for it? Yeah, I don't know about all that.

I began to gather my things when Akeno strolled into the room, put on his coat, and gazed at me.

"Ready, Denice?"

"Huh?" I looked at Ashlynn, who gave me a fake apologetic smile.

"I was just about to head out, too. No need for everyone to go outside to walk us to the car," Ayzo shrugged.

I darted my eyes back to my friend, who mouthed 'sorry' but had a massive grin on her face. I shook my head. Ashlynn's ass wasn't slick. I strolled over and hugged her, but not before pinching her in the arm. She winced with a laugh and nudged me out the door.

I didn't mind if Akeno walked me to my car. I mean, it wasn't like he was going home with me. I scooped up my purse and waved goodbye to my friends before leaving.

We walked in silence until we reached my white truck, which had all-black rims and trimming. Akeno let out a low whistle as he walked around my vehicle.

"Akeno, meet Cruella, Cruella, meet this punk ass boy named Akeno," I smirked at him.

"Your little nicknames for me aren't cutting as deep as you'd like. Speaking of cuts, what happened to your hand?" he nodded.

"Nothing," I exclaimed, moving my hand behind my back.

He arched an eyebrow at me before placing his hands into his pockets and leaning against my truck. "Something tells me that you've visited an old friend, and since the cuts on your hand look fresh, I can only assume it's why you were late getting here tonight."

"Don't do that shit on me!"

"What shit?"

"That creepy, stalker, private eye bullshit you know how to do."

He threw his hands up playfully and laughed. "I apologize, Denice. Sometimes, it's hard for me not to be so observant. Especially when I run into someone in my past that I haven't gotten my mind off of."

I clenched my thighs together to stop the aching pulse between my legs from Akeno's gaze. Desperate to escape his presence, I rolled my eyes and scoffed. "I'm not about to listen to your bullshit. Goodnight."

I hurriedly unlocked my door and hopped into my truck. I backed out of my parking space and drove off, not sparing another glance. Damn him! I was not about to fall for his crap, but I'd be lying if I said I didn't want to feel him again.

When I woke up eight years ago and found that Akeno had left me without a note or goodbye, it crushed me. The little bit of hope I had for giving love a chance was shattered. Of course, I didn't immediately love him, but I saw so much potential with Akeno.

I knew he was different, and I could see myself easily falling for him, but he showed me his true colors. Therefore, I vowed to never allow another man to have me – emotionally and fully sexually.

I pulled into my parking garage and gripped the bridge of my nose. I don't know how much longer I'd be able to face Akeno and try to reframe myself from smashing his nose with my fist.

I was content and living a comfortable life – he was a damn distraction and messing up my simple flow. I took a deep breath and hopped out of my truck.

"It's going to be okay. I can be cordial during our biweekly game nights but continue to avoid him at all costs. He'll get the hint and return back to wherever he'd been for the last eight years. As long as he doesn't try anything and I don't get any more popup surprises, I can get back to my life," I said to myself as I grabbed a pint of double chocolate chip ice cream from the freezer.

    I heard my phone buzzing from my purse as I scooped a spoonful into my mouth. I dug out another scoop as I retrieved my phone, but instantly dropped it to the ground as I read the text message on my screen.

> **Unknown**
> Hey, bighead! It's me, Luther.

Chapter 16

Ayzo

I stared up at the ceiling, observing the blades of the fan spin, causing the cool air to whip through my hair. I didn't care how cold it was outside; I couldn't fall asleep without some fan on, but tonight, it wasn't that easy to drift off.

    I sighed as I ran my hand across my bare chest. Even with the fan on at the highest speed, a belly full of Thai food, and my body sore from an impromptu thirty-minute workout, I still couldn't sleep. My thoughts were plagued with Denice. I should have just told her what happened that night. I mean, maybe I was making it more of a big deal than what it actually was.

I recapped that night. First, my mother destroyed my father's car and tried to run us over while she ran and put a hit out on us when she met up with my uncle. Second, it was confirmed that her foster sister got tossed up a few times by her ex-boyfriend and his friend. Third, Luther threatened that he was going to get rid of me and anyone else who tried to get close to her before he had a chance to have her.

Shit! Okay, now that I've thought about it, that was a wild story that I highly doubt she would believe even though it was the truth. Hell, Luther probably filled her head with all types of bullshit about me hence the reason why she hated my guts. Well, that and I up and left in the middle of the night without a word. To be fair, I did leave her a note with my number, but she never called.

My phone hummed on the nightstand, and I groaned. It was well after midnight – nobody but some female I shamelessly flirted with would be hitting me up at this time of night. I hated spending so much time entertaining women when I had no intention of pursuing anything from them besides conversation. Occasionally, I'd get an urge to do more than talk, but I didn't want just any ole girl.

The night I tasted a sample of Denice's sweet honey, I couldn't find anyone else who was close in comparison. I mean, I finally had sex my first year in college, but once I realized that she nor any of the other girls could ever compare to Denice, I stopped trying.

I hadn't had sex in over six years - I didn't have the appetite to do so. That was until I laid eyes on Denice again; now, she's all I thought about.

I needed her like I needed air, but the shit startled me. One night of passion eight years ago, and she still had my heart fluttering.

My phone buzzed again, and I reluctantly grabbed it. I rolled my eyes as I saw 'bar girl' sent me a text message. Damn, what was her name again?

> You up?

> Kinda. What's up?

> I just got out of the shower and was thinking about you. Are you in the mood for some company?

    I stared at the message and contemplated how to respond. I wasn't going to lie, I was horny as fuck, but I didn't want this random woman - I wanted Denice.

    After a few more minutes of staring at the screen, I chose not to invite her. Instead, I grabbed a hoodie from the closet and a pair of gray sweats. I slipped on my shoes and grabbed the key to the rented Airbnb house I had been occupying. I needed to clear my head. I only made it three blocks before my thoughts drifted to my cousin Seojun. I haven't spoken to him since we came out of hiding together.

    I knew something was wrong when he texted me two years ago to meet him in Chicago. The plan was to support my cousin with whatever dilemma he was going through and then return home to help Nicholas and Garrett do a drop-off. Hell, I was supposed to be in Chicago for only a few days, but things didn't go as planned.

I was bittersweet about the whole situation. A part of me was angry that I wasn't there for Nicholas and Garrett, but it was only by the grace of God that my cousin called me away. If I hadn't been on the plane, I would've ended up with a bullet lodged in me like my friends.

On the other hand, my cousin's empire was demolished, and we spent two years hidden away from the world. Everyone we thought we could trust and who was loyal to our family turned their backs on us. We were outnumbered and had no one to help us, so we ran. Granted, no one really knew my role because they did not know that I was The Shadow, but I wouldn't leave my cousin alone.

I had several burner phones for Seojun and me to contact the few people we entrusted, but we had to keep things brief. At the end of the day, we didn't know who else we could trust besides Uncle Chul-Moo and Nicholas.

I loathed that we didn't know who the mastermind behind my cousin's fall was, but they had better hope I found out before Seojun did. My cousin allowed his plot for vengeance on whomever they were to fuel his anger, and he wouldn't stop until he was satisfied.

***

I knocked on Nicholas and Ashlynn's door and yawned in the back of my hand. After I finished my walk, it was well after two in the morning before I finally went back home and crashed. My blissful sleep was shorten when Nicholas texted me to meet at his house for help. Usually, I would've pretended like I didn't see the text until I got all eight hours of my much-deserved sleep, but Nick was my boy.

I tried to talk my way into meeting for a late brunch, but he insisted I arrive early. Apparently, Ashlynn would be gone with her first hair appointment for the day. Why he was adamant that she had to be gone was beyond me. I still found it strange that they weren't living together. I mean, Ashlynn was at Nick's place damn near every day but was still living with Denice until she found her own place. Oh, well – it wasn't my business.

I lifted my hand to knock again when I heard a soft whimper from behind the door. I arched an eyebrow and stared at the wooden frame. Now, I know I was still tired, but I know I heard a female's moan in there. I placed my ear against the door and clenched my teeth.

"Ahh, fuck baby, tear this pussy up."

"I'm about to cum."

I pounded on the door. Nick may have been my homeboy, but I wasn't about to let him screw up what he and Ashlynn had – she was the best thing for him. Whoever this bimbo was, I was going to throw her ass out.

"Fuck!" Nick grumbled in aggravation, and I could tell I had messed up his flow, but I didn't care.

After a few moments of rustling around in the townhouse, Nick swung the door open with a glare. I smiled at him and opened my mouth to curse his ass out when Ashlynn stepped beside him.

"Good morning Ayzo. I can't talk – I'm already running late," Ashlynn rambled, kissing Nick on the cheek and taking off down the stairs.

I'll chalk up my completely dumbass mistake to my being sleep deprived. I knew better than to think that Nick would do any foul shit. Ashlynn had that man ready to go to war for her over a short period. I shook my head with embarrassment.

"Shit, my bad bro! I thought you said she was gone, and you had some hussy in there."

"Nigga! Why the hell would you think I'd hurt Ashlynn like that? And why would I tell you to come by if I had somebody else here?"

I rubbed the back of my neck, "I apologize for interrupting. I should've known better because I know you wouldn't get down like that, especially not with Lynn. I'm running off of fumes and not thinking clearly."

Nick sighed as he stepped aside, letting me into his house. "You lucky I need your help."

I nodded as I shrugged off my jacket and sat it on the back of the couch. I yawned and placed my forearm over my eyes as I rested my head back. I just wanted to rest my eyes for a few minutes.

"Speaking of, what is so important that you needed my help that you couldn't text me? Or even better, wait until when my ass got some sleep?"

"Denice got you so wrapped that you're already losing sleep?"

I jerked my head up. "What are you talking about? Me and Denice are just -"

"Friends?" he asked, interrupting me. He sat a cup of coffee in front of me and sat on the adjacent recliner.

"She doesn't like me like that. We're cordial – we can be in the same room together without her wanting to karate chop me in the throat."

Nick laughed, "Well, good because what I am about to ask requires you and Denice to work together."

I arched my eyebrow and stared at him. What in the world could he need help with that would require assistance from me and Denice?

"Well, don't leave me in suspense."

"Okay, so you know I've been helping Ashlynn and her dad out around the shops -"

"How's that going, by the way?" I chimed in before taking a sip of the coffee.

"Before, I was so rudely interrupted," Nick continued, ignoring my question. "I've been assisting around the shops and really enjoying myself. It's a new challenge, and it keeps me on my toes. Remember when I told you I felt like I was missing something a few months back?"

"Hmm. Is that when you were trying to take a bus all the way to Vegas to unalive Olivia but soon found out that what you were missing was to let go of your revenge and settle down?" I smugly asked.

"Okay, okay nigga I didn't ask for a recap."

I playfully threw up my hands. "My fault, my fault, I was just checking, but yes, I remember."

"Besides finding Ashlynn, helping out around the shops with her dad has been exuberant. I have many ideas to help bring back lost customers and a marketing plan to expand across the East Coast within five years."

I couldn't help but smile at how Nick's eyes brightened with excitement. When we reconnected a few months ago, the only thing I could see from my friend was hurt and anger. Funny how God works sometimes. Right when you're at the lowest in your life but continue to trust him, he places everything you need right in front of you.

"I'm glad everything is working out for you, man, fo real."

"Thanks, bro."

"Enough of the mushiness – what did you need my help with?"

"Well, Ashlynn has been at Unique's for a minute, and she's built a substantial amount of clients to open up her own shop. Her birthday is in eight months, and I want to surprise her."

"That's what's up! How are you going to do that?"

"I want to build her own salon from the ground up, but I need to find an adequate piece of land - that's where you come in."

"Damn man, you putting us basic men to shame. I thought you were going to ask us to set up a surprise party or some shit," I chuckled.

"Go big or go home. Plus, Ashlynn deserves it. Her dad and I have been discussing getting her salon up and running for her – even though he initially hoped she'd change her mind and work with us. However, once he saw her happiness when she was in her element, he truly accepted that his daughter doesn't want to be in the automotive biz."

"Welp, I'm down! What do you need me to do?"

"I need you AND Denice to check out a few properties for me. I can't really leave the shops, especially with how much business has picked up. Plus, I don't want Ashlynn to get suspicious when she notices I'm leaving often without a valid explanation - you know I can't lie for shit to her."

I bobbed my head as he continued to go over his plan.

"I've already had the blueprints drawn up, and Denice is a freelance interior designer. So, with your familiarity with the area and her eye for decorating, I can have her shop up in no time."

I chewed on my upper lip before clasping my hands together and standing up. I didn't want to sugarcoat what I had to say because I knew that Nick liked blunt honesty.

"I first want to say this is an amazing idea, but don't you think you're doing a lot for just your girlfriend? Don't get me wrong, I have nothing against Ashlynn, and I couldn't be more pleased that you two are together. It's just that this whole idea is a huge deal."

Silence filled the air, and I swear my friend could hear my heart drumming against my chest. Like I said, I really enjoyed him and Lynn together, and I was definitely not hating on them, but what if they broke up? He was about to pour his heart, soul, time, and money into this project—I just wanted to make sure he was making the right decision.

Suddenly, a sly smile danced across Nick's face as he got up and wandered to his bedroom. A few moments later, he returned with a square velvet box. My eyes bulged as I stared between him and his hand.

He nervously chuckled and shrugged, "I love her."

I walked over and gave my best friend a congratulatory hug. I was delighted to see my friend change his life, let go of his past, and find love again. It didn't matter that they hadn't been together a year yet. When a man knows he's ready, he'll act on it.

I patted him on the back and decided to stop ignoring the butterflies in my stomach. I would talk to Denice and pray that she would allow us to start over.

Chapter 17

Denice

I didn't usually work Mondays, but I contemplated opening the office as an excuse to escape this encounter. I don't even know why I agreed to meet him for lunch. The fact that his ass hit me up out of the blue had my nerves bad, and I had a strange feeling that I should have just ignored him.

I shifted in my seat as I folded the napkin in my lap for the tenth time. I tried to look everywhere but at Luther. Unfortunately, I couldn't help but steal a few glances at him.

His rich espresso skin was still littered with tattoos, but he definitely collected more over the years. His pink lips were full and luscious as ever while his once short hair was now in a low, rugged fro that suited him. His sturdy body had lost a bit of muscle over the years, but he was still unmistakably fine.

I sighed and sat back in my seat as the last few hours I had with him, and Akeno raced through my mind. After everything that transpired all those years ago, I never found another guy I could genuinely connect with like I did the pair. Granted, I didn't want a guy who was promiscuous like Luther or played disappearing acts like Ayzo.

"So, how are your folks?" Luther asked.

"Dad Erin died by a hit-and-run driver on my eighteenth birthday, and Mama Julia was so distraught that she ended up passing away a few months later. The doctors said she died of some tumor, but I think it was because her heart was broken."

"Oh shit. I'm sorry to hear that, Denice. I didn't mean to start off the conversation so gloomy." Luther said apologetically.

I shrugged. I was grateful for my adoptive parents, and I did miss them, but I couldn't bring them back. Just like I couldn't get back my birth mother after my dad took her life.

Bile rose in my throat, but I quickly swallowed it down as I took a sip of water. I didn't want to get all emotional, so I bottled down my sorrow – like I always did.

"You look magnificent, Dee. Not that you weren't beautiful before, but you have really grown into a breathtaking woman." Luther complimented as he tried to change the subject.

I gave him a tight-lipped smile and cleared my throat. "Thanks, but cut the crap Luther. Don't you remember I was already a victim of your flirtatious game?"

He chuckled before taking a sip of his lemon water. "Still have that smart-ass mouth that used to turn me on. Hell, it still does."

"Spare me, Luther. Why did you hit me up after all these years?"

"Damn straight to business, huh? Well, I've been traveling between here and Chicago for years, and instead of always having to get a hotel, I bought a second home down here."

I arched an eyebrow. "That doesn't answer my question. Why did you hit me up out of the blue? Hol' up, how did you know I was even in Philly?"

"You have advertisements all over social media. I've seen countless viral videos of how you've completely redecorated multiple different homes and offices. I mean, kind of hard to not know that your main office is out here when you tell people to call you for a consultation."

My cheeks warmed with embarrassment. I was being paranoid because how did I forget about my marketing team and content creators advertising my company? I was used to people coming up to me for business all because of a few videos they had seen. Shit, even my phone number is plastered on my website. It wasn't far-fetched that Luther found me.

"My bad, Luther. It's just weird seeing you after all this time. Besides, it's not like we ended our friendship on a great note."

"I feel terrible about that. I shouldn't have tried to make you my property or threaten you," Luther stated with an ashamed frown.

He opened his mouth to say something else, but we were interrupted by our waitress. She had to be in her early twenties with long blonde hair that was pulled into a high ponytail. Her cheery demeanor eased the tension.

"Are y'all ready to order?" she said in a southern drawl that reminded me of my childhood.

"I'll take a chicken wrap with sauteed bell peppers, onions, and banana peppers. No cheese, please."

"No cheese?" Luther asked with an arched eyebrow.

I shook my head. "Cheese is gross."

"Did you want the avocado ranch with your wrap?" the waitress asked.

"No, ma'am - no dressing."

"I take it you think the ranch is gross, too?" Luther huffed out.

"Yup!"

"You tripping. Hey there, Melinda," Luther said, examining the waitress's name tag. "Scratch what she said and get us both the chicken wrap with everything on it. She needs to at least try it first."

"Excuse the fuck out of me?" I asked in astonishment.

"I said you need to at least try it."

Luther's dark brown eyes pierced through mine, and I could see from my peripheral vision that the waitress had taken a subtle step back. This muthafucka had lost his damn mind if he thought he was going to control what I ate. I opened my mouth to curse his ass out before he shook his head with laughter.

"I'm kidding, I'm kidding."

He gave me and the waitress a smile that didn't quite meet his eyes, which made me feel uneasy. My intuition made an appearance and told me to let this be the last time I met with Luther. The waitress giggled as she placed her hand on her chest. I gave a timid laugh and took a sip of my beverage.

"I'll have what she's having, but you can keep everything on it," Luther winked. The waitress's cheeks displayed a light hue of rose pink before she nodded and commented she'd be back shortly with our orders. Luther stared as she strolled away.

I shook my head in disgust. Apparently, some things didn't change.

Luther glanced back at me and cleared his throat, "So, what are we going to do after this?"

"We?"

"Yes, we! C'mon Denice, we haven't spoken in years, and I want us to reconnect."

"That's why we're at lunch now."

Luther rolled his eyes, "You know what I meant."

"Look, I don't know what else you thought would happen when I agreed to meet you, but this meal is as far as me and you are going to go today." I folded my arms across my chest and sat back in my chair.

"Don't be like that, Dee."

I groaned and grumbled under my breath. "Jeez, why is everybody coming out of the woodwork trying to return to my life."

"What?"

"Nothing."

Luther narrowed his eyes, causing me to shift into my seat. My phone buzzed, giving me the distraction that I needed.

> **Unknown number**
>
> Hey, it's Ayzo; oops, I mean Akeno. I hope you don't mind, but Nick gave me your number. He told me you already know about his plan for Ashlynn and suggested I text you. So, hit me up when you get a chance.

As I read the message, a small smile naturally formed on my lips. That tended to happen whenever the mere thought of Akeno flashed through my mind. Damn him!

When I went over to meet Ashlynn for our workout, Nick pulled me to the side and told me about his surprise. I fell in love with the idea and was so excited for my best friend. Nick was a great man, and I could tell that he really loved her.

So naturally, I was all in to ensure the plan was executed, but then, he told me I would have to work with Akeno. I damn near cursed his ass out, but Ashlynn was my girl, and she deserved to be pampered and loved on. I wasn't about to ruin her surprise because I couldn't swallow my pride to work with Akeno.

"What are you smiling at?"

"Huh? Oh, um, nothing." I stammered as I put the phone back into my purse and coughed.

Shit, I hated that Akeno had so much effect on me. If I were honest with myself, I liked that Akeno was trying so hard to get back into my good graces. I was giving him a hard time, but I just wanted him to tell me the truth. Who knows, maybe I'd be a bit more understanding, but we'd never know if he didn't grow some nuts.

After meditating and praying over the past few months, I realized I was more hurt than angry at Akeno. I was a scared, vulnerable teenage girl and had never felt anything like what we had. Yes, it was only for a day, but it was the happiest day I'd had in a long time.

I didn't know or understand why the two people who had affected my past the most were back in my life. I guess God was trying to show me something. I didn't know what, but I would keep my guard up until I found out.

Chapter 18

Denice

Luther and I finished eating our lunch in awkward silence and small talk. It was only uncomfortable because I was ready to go and not inputting too much into his attempted conversations.

I should've just agreed to meet Luther for a coffee so I didn't have to waste an hour with him. I wasn't trying to be rude, but my mind was preoccupied with Akeno. I was itching to text him back only because it was early enough for us to start looking at properties today. Well, that, and it wouldn't hurt to talk to him.

"So, when can I take you on a real date?" Luther asked, walking me to my truck.

Never, I thought to myself. Okay, I was being cruel, and I'm sure Luther had grown into a mature, respectable man. Still, I really wasn't interested in him. Besides, a small part of me was nagging that I needed to keep Luther at a distance. The shit he said to me all those years ago still sat at the back of my mind, and it was hard to forget.

"I'll have to see. I can get pretty busy between my business and helping with side projects."

"Well, I'll be waiting for your text."

Luther caught my hand and drew me into a hug. He dug his head into my neck and inhaled sharply, letting out a low, throaty growl. I quickly disconnected our embrace and pinched my eyebrows together. Did this fool just really sniff me?

"I'll see you later," I said, springing into my truck.

I waved goodbye before speeding out of the parking lot. I would've waited for him to go to his car but figured he'd be fine. Besides, he was creeping me out, and I no longer wanted to bask in his company.

As soon as I returned to my house, I sat on my couch and texted Akeno.

> Hey, I apologize for the late response; yes, Nick has already told me about his plans for Ashlynn. We can look at the first property today.

> That's a plan. What time do you want me to pick you up?

🙄How about you send me the address?

LOL, it was worth a shot, but there are a lot of properties on Nick's list. It'd be a good idea to devise a schedule to view all of them. I'm sure your schedule gets hectic, especially since you have to manage Dee's Designs, LLC.

You damn right, suga. My baby comes first, but that's why I hired employees to handle the day-to-day business. So, send me the address, and I'll meet you there

That sounds good, beautiful. I'm about to hop in the shower and head that way. Give me a hour.

I slowly dragged my tongue over my top lip with the sheer thought of Akeno – naked. I could feel my pussy soaking with the idea of Akeno's muscular yet slender body dripping wet as the shower sprayed down.

My breathing quickened as I ran my hand down my chest. I teasingly grazed my nipples with the back of my hand. My body ached with need as I laid back on the couch before shutting my eyes. As much as it irritated me that Akeno simulated me like this, I needed to release this backed-up pressure. I mean, it wouldn't hurt to use my imagination, right? Fuck it.

I unbuttoned my pants and gingerly trailed my hand from my breasts to between my legs. I envisioned myself watching Akeno through the glass shower door as the steaming water dripped down his caramel body.

Akeno ran his hands through his curly mane as he slowly licked his lips before biting down. His brown eyes dared me to join him, but I didn't. Not yet. Instead, I sat on the adjacent jacuzzi tub and spread my legs for him to watch me play.

I ran my hand down my chest and caressed my breast, pinching both of my nipples between my thumb and finger. Akeno's honey-brown eyes darkened as he held on to his thick hard dick.

"Let me hear how wet you are, baby," he panted as he slowly stroked himself.

"Mmm," I hummed as I slid my hand in between my legs and rubbed my clit.

I teased and massaged the nub as my fantasy continued to play out in my mind. I threw my leg over my couch and dipped a finger into my tight opening. I wasn't supposed to be doing this. I wasn't supposed to want him, but the thought of his lips trailing down my body had my back arching off the couch. He was so gentle with me before, and I couldn't help but wonder how he'd handle me now.

"Fuck," I moaned, rubbing my pussy faster. Thinking about Akeno like this was absolutely wrong, but it felt so fucking good. I panted as the sensation to orgasm built in my core.

Wait, what am I doing? My brain screamed for me to stop. Why am I getting myself riled up just to be ghosted again? No. No, I can't do this.

"Damn it!" I yelled out in frustration as I dropped my leg and pulled my fingers from my clit.

I let out another frustrated groan before I got off the couch, grabbed a fresh pair of clothes, and hopped in the shower. I closed my eyes and let the water wash over me, wishing it would cool my hot ass down.

While I had never had sex, I still had urges to come now and then, and I was able to handle them. Hell, even when I dated, I was able to practice self-control with my sexual needs.

The only man to have a tiny part of me was back in my life, and now my pussy wanted to be hot and ready. Her dumbass leaked and pulsed with excitement, all for Akeno. Every time Akeno was around, or the mere thought of him made me horny as fuck.

Usually, when I needed a release, I could get myself to that blissful satisfaction without any problems, but lately, it was becoming harder to satisfy myself. I would start off pleasing myself well, but my thoughts always drifted back to Ayzo, and I wouldn't dare cum for him again.

So, I tried to ignore my urges. Unfortunately, the more I tried to ignore my needs, the more I thought about Ayzo and got hornier. Something had to give, or I swear I was going to die of sexual frustration.

What if I gave him another chance to get close to me? I mean, what harm could that do? But then again, what if he disappeared again? Even worse, what if he started to act crazy like how Luther did? They were close friends, and birds of a feather flock together. I was scared to take that risk. Yeah, I couldn't do that again. I…I just couldn't.

Chapter 19

Ayzo

"What's up, Denice? You are looking stunning as usual," I said, opening her truck door to help her out. She wore a simple black sundress and matching black sandals that strapped up her toned legs. She glanced down at her feet; I could've sworn a slight blush had colored her mocha cheeks.

"Thank you, Akeno."

I gasped and dramatically threw my hand against my chest. "What? No insult, or you telling me to go fuck myself?"

She smirked and gave me the middle finger. "Don't flatter yourself—I'm in business mode, and I don't do insults when I'm working."

"So, I'll have to hire you for you to be nice to me – got it."

She laughed; it was the sweetest sound I recalled from her when we were teens. "I have been an asshole to you, huh?"

I shrugged, "I mean, only for the last five months, three weeks, two days, and four hours, but who's counting? I get it, though. I shouldn't have just left you that night."

She flung up a hand and shook her head. "Akeno, let's not get into that today. We will use this time to check out a few properties for Nick so that my best friend's birthday can be spectacular. I promise to not be a complete bitch to you if you can promise to leave the past in the past."

"But I want to tell you everything," I argued back.

"One day. Until then, let's get to business."

I stared at her as she nervously fidgeted. As much as I wanted to tell her, I figured it wasn't worth the bickering. I had a chance to talk to her without the hostility, and I wasn't about to fuck that up. So, I'll do as she asked, for now. Then, she'll have to hear me out.

I nodded my head and stuck out my hand for a handshake. She took it and gave me the businesswoman smile I'd seen in her advertisements.

"Alright, Nick's given us a list of seven potential properties to start building. I've already crossed off two because the area would not be a good fit. It was oversaturated, and we want Ashlynn to stand out," Denice said, pulling out a map of the area.

"Agreed and I crossed off two more because that area may look beautiful during the day, but once the sun goes down, it gets heavily active, and I don't mean in a good way."

"Cool, that leaves us with just three properties. What's your schedule looking like for the next few weeks? I am free on Saturdays and Sundays after church."

"Hey, I'll come running whenever you call me baby."

Denice scrunched up her nose and rolled her eyes at me. She pulled out her phone and opened up her calendar. I watched as she mumbled to herself about not wanting to miss meetings and having an impromptu luncheon with her employees. I beamed at her and rested my elbows on the hood of her car.

"You look sexy as fuck when you get into professional mode."

She huffed, "How original. Most men claim they like independent women but recoil from them."

"I'm not most men."

"So, you like when a woman is in charge?" she laughed mockingly.

"Mm-hmm. Just like how you dominated me when we were watching that scary ass movie," I whispered.

Her laugh was cut short, and I could've sworn a shiver ran up her body. She briefly closed her eyes, and from how her breathing accelerated, I could tell she remembered that night.

I took my chance and stepped closer to her. My chest pressed against her shoulder, causing her to stiffen, but she made no attempts to move.

"Like how you sat on my lap and grinded your hips against me as I bit on your ear. Then you took over by gripping my neck and trailing your tongue down my body."

I slightly lowered my head so my lips brushed her ear. Her breath hitched as I gingerly ran my hand up and down her forearm and took in her sweet floral perfume.

"Akeno," she whimpered in a panting voice that made my dick jump. "We have to be professional."

"I'm not doing anything. Just reminiscing with an old friend."

"Please, don't."

"Don't what?" I breathed in her ear. "You know, I'd still let you take control of me now. This time, I'd let you wrap your legs around my shoulders and have your way with me." A small moan escaped her lips before she clamped her teeth down onto her lower lip. "I bet you taste so fucking good."

I gently flicked my tongue against her earlobe, causing her knees to buckle. She balanced herself by grasping onto the car's hood and tightly closing her legs. By the way she was swaying back and forth, I could tell that she was turned on and trying to ease the pressure building in between her thighs.

She ran her hand up my arm, and my heart began to pound against my chest. Blood pumped through my dick, making it harder by the minute. I licked my lips and decided to show Denice what she was doing to me.

I gently pressed my length against her ass cheek, and a small gasp escaped from her lips. Her hand left my arm and grazed the side of my leg, driving my breath to stutter. If she would give me the word, I would have no problem with laying her down in the backseat of her truck and allowing her to cum all over my tongue.

"I-we can't do this." She shook her head and stepped away from me, a pained look etched across her face as she took in several breaths. Her eyes trailed down to my hard dick, and I could've sworn she was about to start drooling with the way her mouth hung open.

"Stop playing, baby," I cooed, stepping toward her, but she broke her gaze and moved farther away.

"We have to keep this business professional."

I stared at her for a long while before an irritating chuckle escaped from my lips. "How do you expect to do that, Dee? You can deny it, but I know you want me just as badly as I want you."

She smoothed her dress and took a deep breath, her demeanor changing to a nonchalant status. "It's Denice, and I will not participate in the game you are trying to play. Besides, I know how you like to play ghost."

She then turned on her heels and walked away. She shook her head before looking over the map of the first property Nick sent us again. Gotdamn her!

Why was she fighting her feelings when we both knew something was between us? One minute she wanted to talk shit and throw jabs at me, and then the next, she was looking and touching me like she wanted me to bend her over.

Yes, I fucked up in the past, but she was holding that over my head like her life depended on it. She wouldn't even allow me another chance to tell her the truth. I ran my hands through my hair and exhaled.

Maybe it may be time for me to move on and get Denice out of my system once and for all. I've gone years without being around or touching her, so what's a few more weeks? I could control myself long enough so that we could help out Nick, and then I was done. I'd go back to Vegas and help out my cousin to figure out who betrayed him while keeping Denice in the past with my feelings.

"Okay, Denice. It's only a professional relationship from here on out."

We spent the next hour checking out the area, which wasn't that bad. The available land had a neighboring burger restaurant and a candle shop—odd combinations, but there was potential for walk-in clients.

"What do you think about this place?" I asked Denice as we headed back to our cars.

"It's okay, but I highly doubt Ashlynn would want to smell fry grease all day."

I nodded because she had a point. Plus, it didn't help that the candle shop had what I could only describe as interesting smells roaming the area.

"Good thing we have two more spots to choose from." I chuckled but noticed that Denice was scowling at her phone. "What's wrong?"

She turned the screen off and shoved the phone back in her pocket.

"Nothing – just a slight complication from my job. One of my employees who was in charge of handling a sponsorship meeting this afternoon just told me that she had a last-minute emergency and couldn't do it. I'll need to run home and jump on the call, but the file I need is at my office. I don't have enough time to go to my office and prepare for the meeting. Dammit, I should have backed up the file on my laptop."

"I can help. Just let me know where the file is, and I'll get it back to you before you know it."

"Really? You'll do that for me?"

"Of course!"

"But why?"

I shrugged. "I'm not a complete asshole Denice. If a friend or a temporary business partner needs help, I help – regardless of my feelings for them."

She rubbed the side of her arms before giving me a timid smile. "Thank you."

"No sweat! So, what do I need to do?"

"Oh, uh, here are the keys to the building. There is an orange folder right on top of my keyboard on my desk – I'm the only one with a private office. It's the building right on the corner with an attached warehouse right behind it with neon pink lighting. You won't miss it. I trust you won't be a creep and make copies of my keys."

I laughed out loud, "Girl, please. I like you, but not enough to do some off-the-wall shit like that."

She chuckled and gave me the address of her office and her house. I could complete the task in under an hour. I guess I didn't mind going out of my way to help, even though she turned me down again. Who was I kidding? I would have helped her whether I had a crush on her or not. It was in my nature to help when I knew I could. I guess years of doing wrong as The Shadow has made me want to spend the rest of the time I had left on this earth doing good.

Denice and I parted, and within twenty minutes, I was pulling into her office building. It was a quaint space downtown, on the corner of a parking garage and a bookstore. Dee's Designs, LLC hung in neon pink above the building.

I unlocked the door and was welcomed by chic, modern designs. The walls were painted a creamy tan with light pink trimmings along the ceiling and floorboards. Two sets of cubicles were lined up against the wall and decorated with each of her employees' knick-knacks.

Just as she said, Denice had the only private office. As soon as you walked in, right down the middle was a path toward the right where the restrooms were, and Denice's office was on the left.

I stepped into her office and grabbed the orange folder on her keyboard. I turned to leave when I heard a groan. I thought my mind was playing tricks until I heard it again from the bathroom.

What the hell? Why the fuck did I keep running into people that were fucking? I was getting jealous as fuck because I wasn't getting any myself. That was my fault because I only wanted one person; she was just making it difficult as hell.

I quickly returned to the front entrance when a familiar voice echoed from the bathroom.

"You've been such a good girl, telling Denice you had a family emergency. I will take care of you and ensure you get enough money today for the work you miss."

Where have I heard that voice before? A smacking noise echoed, followed by a woman's giggle.

"I feel bad because I've never lied to Denice before. She's always been super understanding, but then again, I could use the extra money and want to help you out, baby."

"Exactly. So, you let me worry about Dee and do what I'm paying you to do. You'll still have a job come tomorrow, but now you'll have an extra stack in your wallet."

"Thank you, baby."

I stood at the door in shock. I had no idea who these people were, but I had a bad feeling. I'm sure the female was Denice's employee who so-called had a family emergency, but who the fuck was the nigga? And, what the hell did he mean he could handle Denice?

Loud sucking and slurping, followed by a low growl, broke my train of thought. I wasn't about to listen to whoever was in there get their dick sucked, but I needed to figure out who he was. Unluckily for them, I knew how to do that.

Chapter 20

Denice

Akeno came through for me right on time. Thanks to him, I had a successful meeting. I was prepared once he provided all the documentation I had left at my office. I ended the meeting with the signature I needed for a one-year contract with the investor.

I sighed and leaned back in my chair. I told my employers from day one that I was a chill boss. If they came to work and proved that the work could be handled with minimum supervision, I'd leave them to it. For a while, that was working. Shit, Jasmine was one of my hardest workers hence the reason I gave her more projects, especially the ones with a commission base. They help grow my business, and I help grow their bank account. Win-win.

I rocked in my office chair and reread Jasmine's text message. Since her family emergency on Monday, she's had four more 'predicaments.' Her ass hadn't come in all week.

As I mentioned, I was pretty understanding about missing work because everyone needs a mental day, or shit happens where you can't make it to work, but I was no dummy.

By now, Jasmine had two sick grandmothers and a sick dog and had gotten a flat on all four tires. I rubbed the bridge of my nose and heaved a sigh. I decided that if she didn't show up on Tuesday, I'd have to start finding her replacement.

My phone dinged with a text message notification, but I ignored it. I barely walked into my office when Jasmine's drama got my nerves bad. My phone chimed again, causing me to let out a frustrated sigh. I saw messages from Luther and Akeno asking if I was available on Saturday. Luther wanted to take me to brunch, while Akeno wanted to check out the next property on the list.

I hovered over the delete button but hesitated. Ignoring the two men disrupting my once quiet life would be easier than responding to their requests to see me. Dammit, I needed advice because right now, I wasn't thinking clearly.

I hit the call button and waited for Ashlynn to answer. She'd know what to do. The phone rang a few times, and I was just about to hang up when she finally picked up—out of breath.

"Uh, is this a bad time?" I asked.

"Hell yeah!" I heard Nick grumble in the background.

"Shut up, bae, I'll be back," Ashlynn giggled. I heard her give him a quick kiss, but by the commotion on the other end, it sounded like they were about to pick up where they left off before I called.

I couldn't be any happier for my best friend. Still, I wasn't up to hearing her getting dicked down, especially since my hormones were going wild ever since Ayzo came back. I was just about to hang up when she cleared her throat.

"Hey girl, what's up? Oh! I forgot to tell you that I saw that new furniture store opening off the toll road and thought about you. Definitely some cute sets to decorate for your clients."

"Oh, right! I almost forgot about that place. I might swing by there -" I cut off my sentence when I heard Nick in the background begging Lynn to hurry up. I laughed. "I'm sorry, Lynn, I know you are busy, but I need some guidance – promise it won't take long."

"Okay, shoot."

"So, I have this friend that recently had not one but now two men from her past pop up, and they're both trying to reconnect with her tomorrow."

"Damn, Dee! Who's this other man?"

"Not me, my friend!"

Ashlynn huffed out a sarcastic laugh, "Right, my bad. So, 'your friend' doesn't know which guy to hang out with tomorrow?"

"Precisely. Both men did her dirty when they were younger but are equally trying to make things right."

"Mmm-hmph. Tell me more about these men." Ashlynn urged.

"We'll call the first guy L. She met him first when her family moved into town. Even though he was a slut, and she's pretty sure he had a threesome with her foster sister -"

"You've got to be kidding! He did what with her foster sister?" Ashlynn shrieked on the other end, interrupting me.

"Lynn, focus."

"Okay, okay, but you'll need to circle back and tell me that damn story later. So, L was promiscuous and got down with your friend's relative. I don't know about him. That is kind of hard to come back from. What's up with the other guy?"

"So, we'll call him A. Now, my friend and A only had a little time together. I'm talking barely a day, but it felt like they'd known each other for years. The connection between them was strong. I mean so powerful that she was willing to go against her morals to give him a chance. Unfortunately, he straight-up discarded her like she was old news after they had one night of sexual exploration. He promised to be around, and they could try again when they were older, but he ends up vanishing on her ass."

"Damn. And I am assuming A didn't leave a note or anything?"

"Nope, he didn't."

"Tsk. There has to be a reason why. I mean, finding a connection like that with someone comes once in a lifetime."

"I'm sure he has an explanation, but honestly, she hasn't given him a chance to explain himself. He tried, but every time he had the opportunity, he froze up or she cut him off."

"I see. Honestly, it seems like your friend can be a bit intimidating and stubborn, especially when someone wrongs her. She has a thick wall up that she's afraid to let down because she doesn't want to feel vulnerable or abandoned again.

I don't know your friend or anything, but I'm assuming she went through a traumatic experience growing up, and she finds it difficult for people to get closer to her. My advice is to hear what L and A have to say. It doesn't hurt to listen. Shit, maybe L and A are both hurting from treating you, I mean her, bad and want to offer closure."

"But she's afraid," I whispered.

"It's okay to be afraid of the unknown. Look at what I just went through - I was terrified of stepping out of my comfort zone. I was willing to put up with the disrespect, verbal abuse, and other crap just because I was content in my surroundings, not caring that it was toxic.

I suggest your friend pray on it and encourage her not to be afraid to step out on faith. There's a reason why God is bringing this test up. Maybe it'll open old wounds that need to be healed instead of them being bottled up."

Tears welled in my eyes as I took in what Ashlynn said. She was right. I was mortified about letting my guard down. I spent years alone because I was afraid of the unknown. The what-ifs of whether someone was overly passionate like my dad or if I was the one who'd snapped made me keep everyone at a distance.

The fear and anger towards my dad and what he did to my mother, on top of the hurt of losing my mother and adoptive parents, caused me to bottle up all of my grief. Maybe it was time that I let the past go. Maybe there was a reason Luther and Akeno were here. What are the odds that they could have been anywhere in the world? Yet God placed them right back in my life when I thought I didn't need anyone else – when I thought pushing everyone away was working.

I let out a shuddering breath before wiping the tears brimming at the corner of my eyes. "I love you, girl – thank you for the advice. Now get back to Nick before he comes to get you."

Ashlynn chuckled, "I love you too."

I disconnected the call and took a deep breath before returning to the text messages. "Okay, Lord, I'm ready for this test," I said out loud.

I texted Luther that he could meet me for lunch at the same restaurant we met at last weekend. Then I texted Akeno to meet me at the bar across the street from said restaurant a few hours later. I was willing to give each man an appropriate amount of my time. Besides, the following property listing wasn't far from the meetup. I wanted to see the area during the day and evening.

My phone chimed with a text notification, and I assumed it was from one of the guys. Instead, it was from an unknown number. My heart pounded against my chest as I read the message several times.

> **Unknown**
>
> You two fat bitches and that alcoholic dumbass are going to pay.

What the fuck?

Chapter 21

Ayzo

I scanned my watch as I sat in the driver's seat of my rental car. It was just after nine, and Denice confirmed she'd meet me tomorrow to look at the next property. I smiled. I was slowly getting back on her good side. We weren't friends, but at least she wasn't cursing me out as much. Besides, I knew she wanted me sexually, just like I wanted her. She could deny it all she wanted, but I told myself I would move on if she kept fighting her feelings.

I didn't want to miss out on meeting my potential soulmate because I was too hung up on the past. It was strange, though. I had no idea what was holding Denice back. Did she already have a boyfriend? Shit, now that I thought about it, I never asked.

It's not like we hung out or spoke outside of game nights before now. Jeez, I was going to feel like a total asshole if she was taken, and I was persistently trying to seduce her. Ugh. Okay, I will figure out what was happening with her employee and this mystery guy, then that's it. I wouldn't text or flirt with Denice anymore and find someone else.

I grabbed my phone and sent Bar Girl a quick message asking what she was doing later. I should've asked her name, but I'd figure it out eventually. She said she was available, and I asked if she wanted to grab some coffee. I exhaled a satisfying breath when she agreed to meet me in an hour.

"Good job, Akeno! You are heading in the right direction to move on with your life, "I said out loud as I patted myself on the shoulder. This date was exactly what I needed to get Denice out of my system, right?

Movement from across the street caught my attention, causing me to snap out of my head and duck in my seat. I watched as the slim, deep, mocha-skinned woman opened her door as someone jogged up the sidewalk to her building. She wore a white crop top and black jean shorts that I'm sure allowed her ass cheeks to hang out of the back. Her long blonde braids swayed down her back as the man lifted her by the back of her thighs and carried her back inside the house.

I stepped out of the car and headed toward the building. After combing through Denice's website and researching her employees, I confirmed that Jasmine was in the restroom with the mystery guy the other day.

I was planning on following her to work in hopes of seeing this unidentified man leaving out her crib, but her ass had called out again. That was cool with me, though. I had both of them right where I needed them. I had no plans to utilize my shadow skills while I was back in Philly, let alone on Denice's employees, but these two muthafuckas were up to something.

I headed toward the back of her rowhome and quietly opened the back fence door. Typically, I was not fond of doing my work during the day, but something was pulling at me to figure out what the hell was going on. Besides, it was the middle of the morning, and the street was quiet. I doubted anyone saw me. I kept low as I heard Jasmine and the man sitting in the kitchen—they must have left the window up.

"Come over here." I heard the man say.

Damn, where have I heard his voice before?

"Bobby, I don't think I can do this. I like Ms. Denice, and she's worked hard to start her company."

Bobby? I knew that muthafucka's voice was familiar. What the hell was he going on? What was he trying to do to Denice?

"I told you; I'm not going to hurt her. I just want my money back. She and my ex's friends robbed me out of a lot of money."

"I know, and I'm sorry that happened to you, baby. I just -"

"Shh, stop thinking," Bobby said in a low voice, cutting off her words.

It suddenly became quiet until the indistinguishable sound of the pair kissing tore through the silence. Soft whimpers echoed through the room before the sound of a chair scraping against the ground pricked at my ears.

I slowly approached the window and observed Jasmine sliding her pants off. She gradually straddled Bobby, easing down on his dick.

"Fuck baby," Bobby groaned as he grasped her waist. "Ride this dick."

She moaned as she rhythmically bounced up and down on his lap. He slapped her ass, causing her to cry out. Bobby held on to her hips as he took over and pounded into her. I didn't want to watch this shit, but I needed more information from these two blabbermouths.

"Just imagine swimming in money, baby. Denice is our best option of getting our hands on all the cash stolen from me and then some."

"Ah yes, Bobby," Jasmine moaned, throwing her head back.

"The best part is, she won't even know what's happening or that you were involved. Shit!" He groaned as Jasmine ground her hips into him. "All you have to do is log in to her account and transfer the funds to our private bank account we set up last month. I highly doubt she'd notice a couple of stacks missing, as much as she brings in. Fuck baby. You like that shit?"

"Yes, yes, yes."

"Tell me you'll stick to the plan," Bobby demanded, thrusting himself so hard into her that her legs began to shake.

"Yes, Bobby. I'll do whatever you want. Fuck I'm cumming." Jasmine yelled as her eyes began to roll into the back of her head.

Her body shuddered and jolted as she held onto Bobby, permitting her climax to take over. A cocky smile formed on his lips as he yanked her off of him. She gaped at him with bewilderment until he clutched a handful of her braids.

"That's what I thought. Now, suck your pussy juice off my dick. Next week, we start, so you better be ready."

My hands balled into fists, and it took everything in me not to kick down the door and fuck their asses up. So, Bobby was pissed that he got fired, and now he was going around saying Ashlynn, Denice, and Nick robbed him? Un-fucking-believable.

I crept back out of the fence and headed toward my car. It was time to get rid of Bobby's dumbass once and for all, but I needed to let Denice know what her employee was going to attempt. Since I am meeting her at the bar tomorrow, maybe I can convince her to drink with me as I broke the news. Who knows, after a few more drinks, perhaps I'll have the courage to tell her what transpired all those years ago.

"One thing at a time," I told myself.

Once I returned to my car, I dug the burner phone out of the middle console and pressed the call button. Since I only called and texted one person on this phone, I didn't need to scroll to find the contact I was looking for.

"My favorite cousin," I voiced when I heard the line pick up.

"Akeno! What's up, man?" Seojun chirped on the phone. "I thought you were only going to go visit out there."

"I know, but that girl I was telling you about -"

"Denice?"

"Yeah. Well, she's here, and I can't leave without her. Not until we at least can be friends again. Besides, one of her employees is trying to steal from her, and I won't have that."

"What do you need me to do?"

"I need you to block out her business accounts – no money in or out without approval."

"Done. I'll call you when that task is complete."

We hung up, and I returned the phone to its hiding spot. When I was training to be the shadow, my cousin was learning not only how to manage the books for all of my uncle's businesses but also learned about the technology behind each system.

Seojun could crack into any cyber security or hack into any software. He was smart as hell and definitely a threat to the other territories, which is why he was still in hiding. I knew it wouldn't be for too much longer, though. We were getting close to figuring out who set him up. Once I got Bobby's ass away from everyone and Nick was able to get Ashlynn's salon started, I was heading back to Vegas to help.

Chapter 22

Denice

I should've listened to myself when I said the last time was the last time I would meet up with Luther. I was just trying to be nice, but this fool was confusing my niceness for me begging for his dick. How that was remotely possible was beyond me.

"I'm glad you agreed to meet me," Luther said, pushing his chair closer. His eyes lingered down my body, stopping at my white button-down blouse. I knew that I shouldn't have worn this damn shirt. I was missing the first two buttons, and there was no hiding this cleavage.

"Right," I said, folding my arms across my chest. "Well, I got some good advice about letting down my guard every once in a while. You were my first friend when I moved to Chicago, and I missed you."

Luther licked his lips and eyed me seductively before leaning into me. "I've missed you too. How about we get the check and head out of here?"

"I meant, "I interjected, "I missed our friendship. After hanging out with you and Xavier so much, it was strange not seeing you two every day."

"Friendship? Dee, baby, we were dating."

"No, we dated - huge difference."

Luther positioned his hand on my leg and attempted to run it up my black pencil skirt. I shoved him away and scooted back in my seat.

"Right." he scoffed. "Well, I've always liked you. I know I was a fool when we were younger, and I didn't understand my feelings for you. I admit that I said some mean and hurtful things that I wish I could take back. Can you forgive me, Dee?"

"Of course, Luther. We can definitely restart our friendship."

"And if I wanted you more than just a friend?"

"Honestly, I just don't have those types of feelings for you. I'm sorry."

"You don't know what you're talking about."

"Excuse me?"

"Dee, how do you think a thriving relationship forms? The foundation is built on companionship. So, since we were already friends, we can start officially dating."

I couldn't hold back the laughter bubbling in my throat. I had to hand it to Luther; that was brilliant. He had a point that we were friends, and I wouldn't mind rebuilding our friendship, but that's as far as I would take it.

"Luther, sweetie, no offense, but I don't want to date."

Luther pouted before snatching away from me and pushing back to his side of the table. He tossed a few bills down before standing up from his chair.

"I'm going to the restroom, and then I can walk you to the car. Hopefully, that gives you enough time to get your mind right."

I rolled my eyes and shooed him away with my hand. He was throwing a tantrum because he wasn't getting what he wanted, but I wasn't surprised. He used to give me that same look when we were younger any time I turned him down. I assumed he had matured, but obviously, I was wrong.

I glanced at the receipt and scoffed. Luther had only left enough cash to pay for his meal. Not that I couldn't pay for my own food and drinks, but damn. He so-called wanted me, but he wasn't even showing any effort outside of trying to get in between my legs.

I reached into my purse and drew out the rest of the money when a piece of paper mixed in with the bills Luther left caught my eye. It was worn out and looked like it had been crumbled up at one point, but the words were still legible. I seized the paper and felt the wind rush out of my body when I saw my name standing out.

Dee, I never intended to leave you, and if I were in a better situation, I would have been there when you woke up. I wish I had more time with you, but I would be worse off if I stayed. I wish I had met you sooner. I'm sorry for ditching you like this in the middle of the night. Even though I'm moving away, I hope you'll remember me. Here's my number. I hope that I'll hear from you soon and I can explain everything. Ayzo.

I couldn't breathe. My chest contracted, and my mouth became dry. I clamped my eyes shut and took slow breaths. My world was turning upside down by the minute.

Akeno did leave me a note! All this time, I believed he just used me, but that was far from the truth. He was trying to tell me why he had to leave that night, but I was so blinded by anger that I didn't listen.

And Luther! How the fuck did he get this letter? Did Akeno ask him to give it to me? It honestly didn't matter because that muthafucka never gave it to me.

The years I spent in resentment against Akeno could've been avoided. Hell, I could've gone to visit him. We could've made a long-distance relationship work. Shit, we could've reconnected as soon as we graduated, but nope. Because of Luther, I missed out – we missed out.

I snatched up my purse off the table and stormed out of the restaurant, not bothering to wait for Luther to come out of the restroom. I didn't want to see or breathe the same air he was in. All of my wrath had been geared toward the wrong person.

I contemplated returning to my truck, racing home, and locking myself in my room, but that was the coward's way out. I would have to face Akeno sooner or later, so I decided to head toward the bar across the street and wait for him. I still had an hour before he showed up, but I could use a more potent drink right about now.

The sun beamed down, but the spring air had a nice breeze that cooled my body. I chose to sit at the bar on the patio and soak up the perfect weather. I ordered a double crown and Coke before reviewing the details about the following property we were about to view to take my mind off everything that had just transpired.

I couldn't believe that I spent eight years believing Akeno was just a fuck nigga that played ghost on me. So many thoughts swam through my head, making me feel dizzy and furious by the minute.

The urge to storm back into the restaurant, kick down the men's bathroom, and stomp on Luther's nut sack nagged at the back of my mind. That fucking jealous son of a bitch. I took several breaths to calm the rage swirling in the pit of my stomach.

Suddenly, I felt someone sit down next to me. I slowly blinked at my drink and clenched my jaw. There were literally open seats everywhere else, but this fool just had to sit next to me. I shook my head. I made the wrong decision by coming to the bar. I was heated, and the last thing I needed was to wind up in jail for hurting an innocent bystander who got trapped in the crossfires of my fury.

I began gathering my things when a breeze swept past, and a familiar cologne took over my senses. The smell of amber, sandalwood, and mahogany had my mouth watering. I inhaled the intoxicating scent while dragging my bottom lip between my teeth. Akeno.

"You're early," I spoke softly, still not looking at him.

I felt so ashamed for treating him like I had, and I ought to apologize, but what if that wasn't good enough? What if he treated me the same way that I have been for the past few months? Who am I kidding? I would one hundred percent deserve it.

"Great minds think alike because I wanted to grab a drink, too. Bartender, I'll have what she's having and put both drinks on my tab."

I finally glanced up at Akeno, and he winked. His beautiful hair was styled into two-strand twists evenly across his head, and you could see his fresh edge up. He wore a white polo shirt that matched his flamingo pink blazer and completed his outfit with a silver chain that hung from his neck.

He tucked his hands inside the pocket of the black designer jeans he had on before flashing his sparkling white teeth at me. Akeno leaned against the bar and roamed his honey-brown eyes across my body. His lustful stare landed back on my eyes as he licked his lips.

"You look good enough to eat Denice. Always so beautiful." His low voice hummed in my ear.

My body warmed, and I could feel my pussy flooding for him. No man has ever had me like this but him. The shit was getting out of hand, but I was afraid to do anything about it. I made myself look like an idiot for treating him like trash – how do I come back from that? I had no idea, but I had to try. I opened my mouth to say something when a low snarl came behind me.

"I didn't dismiss you."

I spun around to see Luther glaring, his eyes pinched together.

"Dismiss me? Do I look like your fucking dog?"

"No, but you're sure acting like a bitch!"

My mouth flew open. Luther had lost his damn mind. The nerve of this muthafucka calling me out of my name. I attempted to stand up to give him a piece of my mind when I felt Akeno place his hand on my shoulder.

"I got you," he leaned over and whispered in my ear before tracing his thumb over my bottom lip.

"Hey nigga, that's my fucking woman! I own her." Luther seethed as he yelled at the back of Akeno's head.

My stomach clenched, and bitterness began to rise in my throat. Luther was acting just like my father – possessive and overbearing. This was why I didn't want anyone to get close to me. Luther and I only dated for three days, but he had become obsessed over me. My heart hammered in my chest. I didn't want to end up like my mother.

Delicate lips grazed my temple immediately making me feel at ease. I peered up at Ayzo, who was giving me a warm smile. How was he doing that? Luther might as well be invisible right now because the way Akeno gazed at me had me on cloud nine.

"Didn't you hear me, muthafucka? I said that's my girl!"

I watched Luther's face transition from irritation to pure hatred as Akeno turned to face him. They stared each other down, and it felt as if time stood still. I held my breath as I examined the two men.

"What the fuck are you doing here?" Luther spat.

"Hoping to pick up where Denice and I left off," Akeno said, arching his eyebrow.

"I told you to stay away from her. Denice belongs to me, or did you forget what I said that night?"

"Oh yeah, I recall that funny joke."

"I wasn't fucking joking around."

"Hell, you could've fooled me, dumbass."

I covered my mouth to hide my chuckle, but it was too late. Luther had already seen me and had his hands balled into fists. I watched as his eyes darkened before he growled and rushed toward us.

I screeched and jumped out of my chair as Luther threw his body into Akeno, but Akeno barely budged from his spot. Instead, he reared his fist back and uppercut Luther in the nose. He stumbled back - blood instantly pouring from his hands as he held onto his face.

"Muthafucka!" Luther yelled as he let out a frustrated snarl.

"Apologize to Dee and get the fuck out of here."

"Fuck you!" Luther spat and charged for Akeno again.

He swung his fist, but Akeno was fast. He dodged every wild punch Luther threw at him. He was so light on his feet like he had been fighting for years. Luther threw another punch, but Akeno ducked down before punching him in the gut. Luther doubled over and coughed as he tried to catch his breath. Akeno brought his knee up and jammed it into Luther's still-bloody nose, rendering him to drop to the ground.

"Fuck the both of yall," Luther murmured as he held onto his stomach in an attempt to get back up. "Denice, you can run all you want, but you know you belong to me! I will be the one to have you – all of you!"

I cringed as he glared at me with his sharp, jet eyes. I stood there gapping at him, not knowing what to say. The same manic look that I saw in my father's eyes when I was eight was gazing back at me again. I was frozen in my spot, just like when I witnessed my father plunge the knife into my mom. A sinister smile spread across Luther's face as he blew me a kiss.

Akeno's jaw clenched before he grabbed my hand and pulled me toward him. He threw a couple of bills on the bar and guided me back toward the parking lot. He didn't let go of my hand, but I did not mind. Instead, I silently prayed and thanked God for opening my eyes.

Luther was disrespectful and delusional. I saw my dad whenever I looked at him and refused to have someone like that in my life. As many red flags that were being waved when Luther came around, I should've blocked his ass from day one. I kept trying to refer to the old Luther in hopes of rekindling our friendship, but I should have left him in the past.

"You okay?" Akeno asked in a low voice.

"Yeah," I stuttered. I wasn't sure that I really was, but I wouldn't tell him that. "Are you okay?"

He shrugged. "Didn't think I'd ever see him again, but that ass whoopin' was long overdue. To answer your question, though, I'm good."

I bobbed my head. Funny how some people act when they can't get what they want. Akeno wanted me, but he didn't act out like a child when I turned him down. He didn't throw a tantrum and say hurtful things. When I looked at Akeno, I didn't feel scared, angry, or uncomfortable, but I felt…at home. He was nothing but kind, gentle, and patient with me, even though I treated him terribly.

I will be the one to have you – all of you!

A shiver ran up my spine as Luther's words tormented me. I should have never agreed to meet him again. I was a fool to believe that he had miraculously changed from the same nineteen-year-old immature boy. He would never have me—intimately or platonically.

I glanced over at Akeno, who had gingerly squeezed my hand tighter. I was going to make things right with him. If he accepts my apology, then maybe we could finish what we started eight years ago.

Chapter 23

Ayzo

I surveyed the dark clouds that loomed overhead. I tried to convince Denice to go home so that she could calm her nerves and avoid the weather, but she refused. Instead, we were checking out the land from the second property on the list. Given how quickly the sky blackened, I realized we wouldn't be here much longer.

This area was two times better than the first spot we visited last week. It was easy to visualize Ashlynn comfortably setting up her salon. The available land had a cozy aura that consoled me the moment we stepped foot on the property. There was a quaint bookstore at the end of the street to the left and a comfy coffee shop to the right.

"Denice, it's about to start pouring – we should head out. I can take you back to your truck."

"Okay, just a few more minutes. I'm in the zone! I can literally see Lynn's entire setup for the shop. A chic modern style salon with a cute waiting area here," Denice beamed, pointing to a section on the ground. "Oh, and a nail technician set up right over here."

I chuckled as I observed her move around the open land, muttering to herself. I loved seeing her face light up with each idea she had. It was like watching a kid at a candy store. Denice stopped in her tracks when lightning streaked the skies, followed by booming thunder.

"Shit!" Denice squealed.

"Come on!" I instructed, pulling her back to my car.

We laughed as rain poured down, drenching us instantly. The playful look on her face had my heart stuttering. I knew I said I was going to give her space and stop pursuing her, but the shit was hard. I even stood up, Bar Girl, because I couldn't get my mind off of Denice. It wouldn't have been fair to waste her time if I wasn't genuinely interested.

I glanced at Denice and watched as she attempted to wipe the water off her face. She eventually gave up when she realized that her damp hair continued to trickle down, declining to stop.

I grinned and couldn't help but wonder how our lives would be if she allowed me to court her. She had everything I liked in a woman—funny, assertive, a bit stubborn, sexy, and independent. She was goal-oriented and wasn't afraid to go after her dreams. I wanted nothing more than to be by her side, but she wouldn't let go of the past and persisted in pushing me away.

Our phones started signaling the tornado watch alert, causing us to flinch.

"Shit, we'll need to get to a secure place asap," Denice muttered, reading the alert.

"I could take you to your vehicle, but it may be too dangerous for you to drive home."

Denice bobbed her head in agreement but didn't meet my eyes.

"Look, I'm renting an Airbnb about five minutes from here. We can wait out the storm, and then I can take you back to your truck."

I watched as she nibbled her lip. The rain, still leaking from her hair, dripped down to her now see-through white blouse. I inhaled a sharp breath and slowly blinked before averting my eyes to her face. I could see the outline of her bra, and if I were to turn on the overhead light, I'd get a perfect view, but I wasn't about to be a perv.

"I-I don't know, Akeno," Denice whispered.

"I promise I won't do anything you disapprove. Hell, I'll stay on my side of the house, and you can stay on the other side if that makes you feel more comfortable. I only want to get us to safety in case a tornado hits."

She fidgeted in her seat but finally nodded her head in understanding. I dipped my chin and headed toward the house. I wasn't lying when I said I'd leave her alone during the storm. We were finally able to be around each other without her insulting me or rushing to get away from me, and I didn't want to mess that up.

Just as I said, we pulled into the garage of the three-bedroom house I was renting out within five minutes. I contemplated getting an apartment out here to save money, but I had no idea what I wanted to do with myself. I had only come down to visit six months ago, but here I still was.

A part of me wanted to stick around to help Nick and Ashlynn's dad at the shops. Then again, why would I linger just to keep myself busy? At the end of the day, there wasn't a reason to stay in Philly.

"There's a bathroom down the hall to the right. My room is at the end of the hall, but any room you choose is yours until the storm passes. Are you thirsty?"

"Thanks Akeno. Um, do you have any whiskey? I could use another drink."

I laughed, "Of course."

She nodded and roamed around the living room, looking at the furniture. That girl was always in work mode, but I get it. Sometimes, it's hard to turn it off when the muse creeps in.

I used to get like that when I first learned to be The Shadow. My ass was using my stealth skills and getting into all types of shit that I had no business with around my house and neighborhood.

I remember practicing my skills by offering my services to other kids in my neighborhood. From getting the class test answers and selling them for a dollar to figuring out what you were getting for your birthday, I was the kid to hire and get the job done.

The more I was hired by my peers, the more I enhanced my skills. I even had one of the teenagers come down and hire me to find out if her boyfriend was cheating on her—which he was. She gave me double what I was charging and gave him a black eye. He was so confused about how she found out because he was careful not to get caught. Of course, he never found out it was me, but he learned not to cheat again.

I chuckled at the memory as I poured our drinks and realized that Denice was staring at me.

"What's so funny?"

"Just reminiscing on when I first learned my, as you call it, private eye skills. I was only about ten."

Her eyebrows shut up to her forehead. "Ten? Most kids that age were playing sports or just hanging out with friends. While you were –"

"Training with the most skilled professionals on how to fight and be the shadow," I chimed in before sipping my drink.

"The shadow?"

I nodded. "Or a dangerous private investigator. I was hired to get vital information from others who usually used what I found for blackmail."

"But you were only ten years old!"

"I started training at ten, but -." I shrugged, "I was willing to do anything to get my mother to love me. If that meant getting jumped into a life that was extremely dangerous and could've gotten me killed if I was caught, then so be it."

"That's why you were so good at fighting and how you got all of those documents on Bobby. As a kid, you put yourself in dangerous situations, all for your mother's love?"

I swallowed the lump in my throat and nodded. A pained look flashed across Denice's face as she sipped her whiskey.

"I just wanted to be normal growing up, but being normal was frowned upon. Why be normal when you can have power and money? I wanted whatever my mom wanted for me. Too bad I was never on that list."

Denice walked around the counter and wrapped her arms around me, resting her head on my back. "I'm sorry, Akeno. No child should ever have to prove their worth or love to get their parent's affection."

I closed my eyes and let out a long, shuddering breath. The genuine sadness in her voice made my eyes burn from the tears trying to well.

"Akeno?"

I sniffed and cleared my throat, "Yeah?"

What happened that night – when you left?"

"When I got out of the car, I spoke with my cousin and affirmed that I wanted out of the Jaguars, the group my mom threw me in. I didn't want to be The Shadow but instead be a normal teenage kid. That pissed off my mom, but I had made up my mind. It must've triggered some chain reaction because my dad found his courage and told my mom he was leaving. He didn't want to be battered by her anymore, and he had found a woman that made him happy. Granted, it was her best friend, but he wanted out of the marriage.

I had to choose between living in an abusive home with my mom or being able to start over with my dad. The choice seemed obvious, but I met you, and for a brief moment, I thought about staying. I was willing to endure the bullshit if it meant that I got to spend time with you, but then, my mom tried to get me and my dad killed."

I felt Denice balk, and her arms wrapped tighter around me. I chuckled and patted her hands.

"It's okay. My cousin was not allowing that shit. It took some convincing and a whole lot of money, but he was able to calm my mother down. My uncle didn't care either way as long as she was happy." I paused and took in a slow breath. "I intended to come over and spend one more night with my friends before I had to move, but it ended up being just me and you. I wanted to leave and find the others, but I was drawn to you from the moment our hands touched that bag of chips. All I wanted to do was be in your company, even if that meant it would only be for a night."

"I had no idea, but that was my fault because I never gave you a chance. If I would've known..." her voice trailed off as she dug her face into my back. "I'm so sorry, Akeno. Ugh! Fucking Luther!"

I spun around with an arched eyebrow. What the hell did he have to do with anything? She ran her hand through her damp hair before digging into her pocket and pulling out a tethered piece of paper.

"That bastard had this the entire time! I should've believed you when you said you left me a note. I should've listened to you, but instead, I was a mean, horrible wench towards you."

I examined the worn letter. How did Luther even get it? Did he come into her room and see it? I opened my mouth to ask but saw Denice hanging her head in shame. I tilted her head back and brought her eyes back to mine. She exhaled a quaking breath as I leaned into her, allowing my lips to brush hers.

"The past is in the past, Dee – let's start over right now," I whispered.

She nodded, "Okay, Ayzo."

With that, she stood on her tiptoes and kissed me. Her lips were so soft and plump, just like I remembered. I tucked my hands under her thighs and lifted her up without breaking our kiss. I carried her into my room as she broke our kiss and started biting on my jaw and down my neck.

"Shit, Dee. That's how your ass got me the first time." I groaned.

She giggled and continued biting me until I slowly let her back down onto her feet. Her eyes darted between me and the bed as she rubbed a hand down her arm.

"I-uh-I don't think you'd want to do this," she said in a low voice.

"Why not?"

"I won't be any good."

I furrowed my brows together and stared at her anxious face. "Why do you think that?"

She huffed out a sound between a nervous laugh and a hiccup before smacking her lips. "I'm a damn rookie - a newbie!"

"You're a rookie? So, you're telling me you've only done this a few times? "

She shook her head. "I'm saying I've never…"

Her words trailed into the loud silence as her face grimaced with mortification. I couldn't help the smile spreading across my face.

I pulled her into me with an embrace. "Can I be your first, Dee?"

Her glazed eyes stared into mine as she nibbled on her lips. She slowly blinked and finally nodded, causing me to pull her into me and dive us into a deep, passionate kiss. Tears streaked down her face as she wrapped her arms around my neck.

"You're mine, Dee. I'd move mountains for you and hurt anybody that tries to fuck with you. Do you hear me?"

She whimpered and nodded as I bit down on her neck. Dragging my tongue from her ear down to her collarbone, I hauled us down until we reached the bed. I dreamt of having Dee back in my arms, and I honestly thought I missed my chance. Now that she was back, I wouldn't let her go.

Chapter 24

Ayzo

I ripped off her white blouse, enjoying the sound of the buttons scattering across the floor. I gazed down at her full breast, barely covered by a lavender lacey bra she wore. It had a silver hook at the front that made my dick pulse with the thought of how swiftly I could have one of her nipples in my mouth. A mere flick of the latch and her delicious breasts would be free for the taking.

I licked my lips and yanked my shirt over my head before sliding down the bed, pulling her black pencil skirt with me. She lifted her hips, allowing me to entirely remove it. Letting the skirt hit the ground, I held her left leg. I traced my finger around the strap of her heels before trailing my tongue up her calf.

"Mmm, Ayzo."

I grabbed her other leg and mimicked the movement, enjoying her squirming in my hands. I kissed and licked up her legs to her thighs until I was eye-to-eye with her matching lavender lace panties. I could smell her arousal seeping through, and my mouth watered. I ripped her panties off her, causing her to gasp.

"Ayz-" my name got caught in her throat and was replaced with a gasp as I dragged my tongue up her center.

"Damn, you taste so fucking good," I mumbled against her lips.

I hummed as I continually sucked and flicked her clit. She gently massaged the back of my head and moaned.

My dick bulged in my pants, and the need to relieve him from my jeans was becoming imperative. I unbuttoned my pants and pulled my dick out, and began to stroke as I started drawing the alphabet with my tongue against her.

"Ay-Ayzo," she panted, her legs trembling with pleasure. "Please, I can't take much more."

"Hol'on baby, I'm only on M."

Her moans and pleas had me harder than a brick, and I could feel pre-cum oozing out the tip of my dick. I didn't want to cum yet, but I wasn't about to stop enjoying my meal.

Once I made it to Z, her legs clamped around my head, and her back was arched off the bed. Her sweet nectar flooded my mouth, causing my eyes to roll in the back of my head as I licked up every drop of her essence. Gotdamn she was tasty as fuck. I planted gentle kisses as her breathing settled and her body began to come down from its high.

"Now I need to do cursive," I declared, diving back in between her legs. I swear, I could suck and lick on her for hours and still not have enough. I only made it to J before she pushed my head back.

"Damn, your tongue is magical - you were about to send me into an orgasmic coma."

I laughed as I kneeled over her, licking her juices off of my lips. Her chest heaved as she stared down at my full, erect length. Her mouth parted as I held on to my shaft.

"Are you sure you want to do this?"

"I want to feel you inside of me," she said in a breathy voice as she wetted her lips.

I briefly closed my eyes and breathed through my nose because this woman was about to make me bust, and I hadn't even been inside of her yet. After mentally demanding my dick not to cum yet, I climbed on top of her.

I kissed her deeply as she wrapped her arms around my back. The tip of my dick gently grazed over her opening, and I let out a moan from how slick and warm she was. I looked at her and ran my hand down her face. I could feel her body trembling as she gazed up at me.

"I won't hurt you baby. If you want me to stop, I'll stop."

She smirked before thrusting her hips up, allowing her wetness to coat the tip of my dick. "Shut up, Ayzo, and fill me up."

I chuckled and captured her bottom lip between my teeth before kissing her. I slipped my tongue into her mouth, and she hungrily sucked it. I groaned as I held my shaft and slowly guided my dick inside her.

I held my breath as I broke past her barrier. She dug her nails into my back as her pussy stretched around my dick. Her body quivered as she let out quick, shallow breaths.

"You okay, baby?" I asked, sitting still inside of her. I hoped that she was because I needed to move soon. She was so wet and tight - I was fighting hard not to climax.

She whimpered, "Stings a bit, but it doesn't hurt as much. Go ahead."

I nodded as I slowly moved in and out of her.

"Fuuucckkk Dee," I moaned out, her pussy gripping my shaft.

The stinging must've subsided because she began matching my movement and rocked her hips to meet my thrust.

"More, please, harder," she cried.

I threw both of her legs over my left shoulder and thrust deeper inside of her as I held onto the headboard. Her blissful cries echoed throughout the house while lightning flashed across the sky.

When I first rented this place, I hated having the big double-paned window in the bedroom uncovered, but now I could see the effect. I was deep inside the woman I cared so much about as the rain pounded against the window. Each time lightning came, I got a glimpse of Denice's pleasure-filled face, which motivated me to drive harder in her.

I was mesmerized by the way her breasts slapped against each other as I continued to hit her G-spot. I leaned down and captured her nipple into my mouth and sucked. My eyes rolled as my core tingled and my balls tightened. I was close, and by the way, Denice's pussy was constricting around me, I knew she was too.

"Shit!" I howled as I pulled out of her and stroked myself until I busted onto the bed. She whimpered as I continued to hold onto her legs and kiss each of her calves.

"Roll over, baby," I demanded, sitting her legs on the bed. I wanted more. Hell, I wouldn't complain if she let me fall asleep in her pussy.

She looked at me nervously before nodding and rotating onto her stomach. I pulled her hips so that she was resting on her knees - her ass on full display before me. I bent down and kissed her ass cheeks, followed by a small bite. She giggled and squirmed underneath me, and my dick was hard and ready for her again.

I held my dick and rubbed the tip back and forth from her opening to her clit. Her back arched as she pushed against me, waiting for me to slide into her wet slit. I groaned as I allowed her walls to stretch for me again and absorb my dick.

"Ah, shit Dee, I could stay in you all day and night," I moaned.

"Yeah? You like this pussy?"

"Fuck yes."

"Be still."

I pinched my eyebrows in confusion but did as she requested. The next thing I knew, Denice started rhythmically moving her hips and threw her ass back against me. Her body moved to her own personal beat like she was dancing, and I was stuck in a trance.

"Gotdamn," I growled, slapping her ass.

When BeatKing said, 'I bet she can't do it on a dick,' he hadn't met a woman like Denice. Baby was twerking her ass back so fucking good, causing my toes to curl - I would have never guessed this was her first time. I placed both hands behind my head and watched her juicy ass bounce and swallow up my dick.

"You taking control again?"

"You like it when I'm in charge," she mumbled, bouncing harder.

"Shit, yes, baby." I could feel my lower abdomen fluttering, and I knew that my second nut was on the horizon.

Denice slightly lifted and wrapped her arm around my neck, tugging me closer to her. I grabbed her hips and drove my dick inside of her. She smashed her lips into mine as she fucked me back. Her kiss became desperate as she moaned on my lips. She was close to her climax, and so was I. I reached up and pulled on her nipple and sucked down on the sensitive spot on her neck.

Her body convulsed, "Oh, Akeno, fuck, I'm cumming."

My stomach clenched with the sound of my name on her lips and her juices spilling down my dick. I held onto her hips tight and allowed her pussy to milk me. We collapsed on the bed and caught our breath. I drew her closer to me and watched as the rain continued to pour down against the window - I wanted to stay right here in this moment forever with her.

Chapter 25

Denice

I fluttered my eyes open and realized I had fallen asleep listening to Ayzo's heartbeat and the constant patter of the raindrops. I never guessed I would be back in the same bed with him after all this time, but here we were.

My body conformed to him like we'd been together for years, and I was glad he was my first. I knew one thing: as soon as I got back home, I was going to throw my toys away. Nothing was wrong with them, but they had nothing on Akeno. I received the first dose of his drug, and I was already addicted.

I idly played with the few strands of hair on his chest as I replayed our conversation before we fell asleep.

"What were you afraid of, Dee? Why did you keep pushing me away?" Ayzo had asked me in a sleepy voice.

"I didn't want to fall for anyone that could be just like my dad. And, I didn't want to ruin someone else's life if I would've turned out just like him."

He peeked down at me with confusion plastered across his face. I took a breath and told him what happened to my parents. I explained how that event altered my idea of love. If there was a chance that my love could drive someone or even myself to the point that murder-suicide was likely and could possibly succeed, then I'd pass on it.

"Dee, baby, you may have the same genes as your parents, but you are not them. Yes, what happened was tragic, and my heart aches for what you had to endure, but you can't assume history will repeat itself. I can't explain why things happen the way they do, but I've learned to trust God, especially during the hardest storms."

"It's just hard to do sometimes, Ayzo. How can I trust God after everything that's transpired?"

"I know it's hard, but don't give up on God because he won't give up on you. Remember what he said: For my yoke is easy, and my burden is light. Let go of your troubles and allow him to handle it for you."

I snapped out of my trance when I heard my phone ringing from the kitchen. I groaned, not wanting to move, but it may have been Ashlynn checking on me and knowing my best friend, she would keep calling until I answered.

I quietly hopped out of bed and made my way towards the front of the house. I grabbed my phone but hesitated as an unknown number displayed on my screen. The text messages and calls from earlier flashed through my mind. Who the fuck was harassing me? Why now? I haven't had any problems with people playing on my phone, but it is now reoccurring.

My hands trembled as I hit the green answer button.

"H-hello?"

"Bitch ass hoe, think you could stop our plan? Think you can send over your dog to spy on us? Well, you got another thing coming." A raspy voice said on the other end. It sounded like a female, but I couldn't be sure. They had the receiver covered, and everything sounded a bit muffled.

"What? Who the fuck is this?"

The person on the other end cackled, causing a shiver to run up my spine. "I hope they make it in time."

"What?"

Before I could get an answer, my line beeped, indicating the call had ended. Who the hell was that? What plan were they talking about? My mind raced with questions, and I could feel myself becoming dizzy.

I didn't have time to process anything else when my phone rang again. This time, the unique ringtone dedicated to my shop's alarm company echoed through the room.

My heart pounded with every possible disaster. I took a deep breath and tried to calm my nerves. Maybe I was overreacting. I mean, my alarm was sensitive and had a glass break sensor—it was common for my alarm to trigger, especially during brutal thunderstorms.

I answered the phone and quickly gave the alarm operator my security code, indicating she was speaking to the owner.

"Thank you for your password, Ms. Hintson."

"What's going on?

"We received a trigger alert about the glass sensor going off, and protocol is to call to verify that everything is alright."

I let out a breath of relief, "Oh yeah. I've had that happen before-"

"I'm sorry to interrupt Ms. Hintson, but we are receiving multiple alerts from the smoke detectors in your building. We are sending over the fire department now to check it out."

My heart plummeted, and I didn't hear anything else the alarm dispatcher had said. I dropped my phone and dashed back to the room – gathering my clothes.

"Shit, what's going on, Dee?" Ayzo grumbled, rubbing his eyes.

"Something's wrong at my shop. The alarm company just dispatched the fire department."

I cursed as I attempted to put back on my shirt but realized all of the damn buttons were dispersed across the room.

"Oh, shit," he said, jumping out of bed. "I'll drive you."

He walked over to his dresser and handed me one of his T-shirts. I wanted to protest because was no way that my titties were going to fit, but beggars couldn't be choosers. Surprisingly, his simple white tee wasn't as tight as I assumed. I pulled on my black pencil skirt as Ayzo threw on a black tee and a pair of gray sweats.

Fear wasn't the closest thing to describe how I felt as Ayzo raced down the highway toward my shop. Between the crazy-ass caller threatening me and the dispatcher causing distress that there might be trouble at my business, I was overstimulated and overwhelmed. Why was this happening? Hell, what exactly was happening?

Just six months ago, I was living peacefully. Then, my best friend went on a wild road trip that ended up bringing back the one man I didn't think I'd ever see again. Like a domino effect, Luther popped up out of the blue and tried to force himself into my life, and now I have some crazy stalker calling me from unknown numbers with threats. How can things get any crazier?

We turned the corner and were on the street of my business when a cry broke out from my lips. Golden flames and dark gray smoke licked the sky as my shop was engulfed.

I didn't wait for Ayzo to stop as I jumped out and ran full speed toward my company. A fireman blocked me from getting any closer, and I felt my knees give out. Suddenly, I was caught by the waist as I wailed in horror.

Ayzo held me and ran his hand down my back as I cried violently into his arms. Everything was gone – the entire warehouse plus my office was in flames. My blood, sweat, and tears were poured into my business, and now I had nothing.

"Shh, shh, baby, I know. I'm sorry," Ayzo whispered into my hair as he tried to soothe me.

"Are you Ms. Hintson?" one of the firemen asked, slowly approaching.

I bobbed my head.

"I apologize for your loss, ma'am. We got here as soon as we got the alert, but the flames had already begun to spread. We believe lighter fluid or some alcohol may have accelerated the fire, allowing it to spread faster than usual."

"So, someone purposely started the fire?" Ayzo asked with a clipped tone.

"We are still investigating, but it is likely. Also, someone in the building unfortunately did not make it out in time."

My head shot up in confusion. "What? Who? My shop was closed this evening."

"Well, we are not certain of the identity and will know after an autopsy. However, a purse was found with the corpse with a photo ID to a," he flipped open his miniature notebook, "Jasmine Wells."

My eyes bulged, and I could feel my throat squeezing. My breathing became short pants as I tried to suck in the air, but I couldn't. The last thing I saw was Ayzo's concerned face as everything turned black.

Chapter 26

Ayzo

I paced back and forth with outrage in the hospital waiting room. Denice had passed out after she witnessed her shop turn into ashes. They wanted to run a few tests before anyone could go see her, hence why my ass was roaming around the area looking like a madman.

I was going to fuck up whoever did this to her. My first thought went to Bobby, but he was weak. He may talk a big game, but the muthafucka was scary as hell, and I didn't think he'd have the guts to pull this type of shit off. Plus, his mole, Jasmine – may she rest in peace, was dead.

I heard them plotting to access Denice's bank accounts and steal money from her. Granted, I had my cousin freeze her accounts. Denice still had access to them, but he was able to kick out any other IP address that didn't specifically connect to Denice's. Also, each interaction required a distinctive code to access the money – which I had and would give to Denice.

So, I ruled Bobby out. He lost his only connection to Denice's money. Who else could have done this? Who was targeting Denice?

I sighed while running my hand through my coils and slumped in one of the uncomfortable chairs. I needed to figure out who did this, but I didn't want to leave Denice. I had called Nick and Ashlynn, who were on the way, but still, I wanted to be the first one at her side when we were finally permitted in the room.

"Ayzo?"

I shot my head up to see the older woman hesitantly smiling at me. She had bags under her dark brown eyes, and her salt-and-pepper hair was pulled back into a bun. Her tiny body seemed fragile under the pink floral dress she was wearing, but she looked stronger than the last time I saw her.

"How are you doing, Ms. Avery? I didn't know you volunteered at the hospital," I said to Nick's mom, nodding at her name tag.

A small smile formed on her lips as she nodded. "Yeah, I've been coming here for a few weeks now. It was only supposed to be a one-time event as part of the rehabilitation program I've been attending, but -" she shrugged her shoulders. "I've enjoyed volunteering – it helps keep my mind off…bullshit."

"That's actually really good. How long have you been sober now?"

She squared her shoulders proudly, "four months."

I smiled as I stood up from my seat and embraced her. I knew Nick despised his mother, but she was trying to change her life. Being sober in a time when getting your choice of poison was as easy as going to a vending machine was an accomplishment—she had every right to be proud.

"Well," she said, wiping a tear from her eye, "I don't want to bother you much longer, and my AA meeting is due to start within the hour. Can I ask one thing from you, Ayzo?"

"What's up?"

"When you see Nicholas, tell him thank you. He's put up with my stupid ass for so long, and I've done nothing but hurt him and Garrett," she visibly swallowed as a lone tear fell down her cheek. She swat it away. "I know I can't change the past, but I'll try to make things right with him until God calls me home. I would tell him myself, but he doesn't want anything to do with me, which is understandable."

I placed my hand on her shoulder. "You and I both know how stubborn Nicholas is. It will take him time to forgive you, but he will. I'll make sure to pass along your message."

She gave me a sad grin, pain, and regret looming in her eyes. She nodded and strolled out of the building as I sat back in my seat. She had a long road ahead of her to fix all of her mistakes and try to regain Nick's trust, but I could tell she was serious about trying.

"Mr. Yi?" A tall black man wearing a white coat and black scrubs called out. He had a stethoscope hanging from his neck and a clipboard in his hand. The name tag pinned on his jacket read Dr. June. Seeing a black man as our doctor made my heart feel at ease. No offense to anyone else, but I always felt comfortable seeing other black people in a field lacking diversity. I may have been mixed, but I cherished my black roots.

I jumped to my feet and headed towards him. "Is Denice okay? Can I see her?"

The doctor chuckled. "Yes, Denice is doing just fine. She had a combination of panic and anxiety attacks that caused her to hyperventilate and pass out. Granted, she did tell me what happened to her shop," a sad look came across his face as he patted my shoulder.

I gave him a slight grin. "Thanks for your concern, doc. Is there anything else?"

"She was also dehydrated and had a vitamin D deficiency, but other than that, she is perfectly fine. We ask that she try to take it easy for a few days. Still, with her current circumstances, maybe someone can be delegated to handle what's happened with her business. Just until she can handle it without feeling those attacks again."

I nodded, "Can I see her?"

"Of course. Nurse Linda," Dr. June called over his shoulder. "Can you please escort Mr. Yi to room 278? The Wells family is here, and I must speak to them."

I glanced over my shoulder and saw a couple in their early fifties sitting patiently in the corner of the waiting room. I was so caught up in my own thoughts that I didn't even realize they were there. My heart ached for them. Yes, the girl was plotting to steal from Denice, and I wanted to rough her up, but I didn't want her dead.

I said a silent prayer for her and her family as I followed the nurse to Denice's room.

Chapter 27

Denice

Somebody planted a target on my back, and I was going to figure out who the fuck it was. First, the unwanted text and calls, then my damn business? Something had to give, or I was going to lose my damn mind.

I took a slow, deep breath. The doctor told me that I needed to stay tranquil, or I would be confined to this hospital bed longer than was necessary.

"Okay, Dee, think. What is different now? Who or what is in your life that wasn't six months ago?" I thought out loud.

Just then, Ayzo walked into my room with a bright smile, and I couldn't stop the nagging voice in the back of my head declaring I had found the culprit.

I mean, a lot of shit has happened since he just popped back up in my life. Things were quiet before Ashlynn brought Nicholas and Ayzo around, and business was as usual. Now, all of a sudden, all hell broke loose — coincidence? I think not.

"How are you feeling?" he asked, strolling to me.

"Fine," I snapped, causing Ayzo to stop in his tracks. He arched an eyebrow as a look of concern spread across his face.

"Dee, are you oka -"

"Was this all a part of your plan?"

He opened his mouth before clamping it shut, followed by a huff of breath. "Dee, what the hell are you talking about?"

"Was this a part of your plan? Lure me in, seduce me, get me until I was vulnerable again, and then get your revenge?"

"Revenge on what?"

"I don't know! About how I've been treating you?"

"How could you even suggest some shit like that?"

I let out a frustrated breath, "I find it mighty funny that ever since you showed back up, I've had nothing but problems. Shit, for all I know you and Luther —"

My words trailed off as realization hit me. It was all making sense now. First, Akeno shows up, and then Luther's crazy ass. The two friends that I met previously who've both seduced me in one way or another just so happens to be in my face eight years later — again, I say, coincidence? I think the fuck not!

For all I know, it could have been one of their girlfriends calling and threatening me. From the types of women that hung around Luther and, I assume, Akeno, I wouldn't be surprised if one of them burned down my shop out of jealousy.

I remember seeing two girls fist fighting in high school when they found out that they were both fucking Luther. One of the girls ended up in the hospital after having her head slammed into the lockers.

"What kind of sick, twisted game are you and Luther playing?" I snarled.

"What the fuck are you talking about?"

"You two have always been close friends. Was it y'all plan to take turns? I let you fuck, and then, unintentionally, after you disappeared again, Luther would've been there to be a shoulder to cry on, allowing him to get his turn?"

Ayzo's nose turned up with disgust as he eyed me up and down. "The fuck, Dee?"

"Did one of your girlfriends get jealous and decide to torch my business?"

"You are talking out of your ass. I will chalk it up to you still being in shock with everything that's happened tonight."

I scoffed.

"Look, baby, I know you are going through a lot right now, and I am sorry for what occurred to your business, but don't take your anger out on me."

"First, you two bombard me, then that psycho trick keeps calling my phone – I can't take this," I mumbled to myself.

"What? Someone has been actually harassing you?"

"One of your girlfriends!"

"I'm being serious, Dee."

"Ayzo, it's none of your concern. I don't know what to think or who to trust right now. Please leave me alone."

"Dee, baby —"

"Just go!"

Ayzo's jaw clenched before he sighed a defeated breath and turned to leave the room. He suddenly stopped and glimpsed at me over his shoulder.

"I know you are scared, but remember what I told you. You can't keep pushing people away because you think history will repeat. You are not your dad." His eyes glazed over as he left the room.

I stared at the door as my mind raced before I grabbed the pillow from behind my head and let out a muffled scream. Why was this happening to me? I was living my life, not bothering anyone, staying in my own damn lane. The minute I let my guard down, unwanted drama sprinted down my path. Yes, I was scared, but all of these events only proved that I needed to keep people at a distance.

Suddenly, my phone began ringing, and I could feel my heart hammering in my chest. I contemplated letting it ring, but curiosity got the better of me. Besides, if it was that damn stalker again, I was going to figure out what the hell they wanted from me. I didn't desire Akeno or Luther — I just wanted my old life back.

"What do you want now?"

"Aw, did poor Denice become so petrified that she fainted and is now in the hospital? How pathetic! You got what you deserved, and now Ashlynn and Nicholas are next."

"Who the fuck is this?" I barked, but my question was unanswered when the call ended.

Before I could process what the hell had just happened, my phone rang again. My jaw clenched as I gripped it so tightly I thought it would shatter. I frowned as Luther's name flashed across the screen. Shit, I thought I blocked his ass after everything he said yesterday.

I didn't want to talk to him, but then I thought about it. I deserved an explanation of what he and Akeno were up to. I wanted to know the truth – no more games.

"Dee, baby girl, I am so sorry about your business. I just saw what happened on the news. Are you okay?" Luther spoke gently as soon as I answered the call.

I rolled my eyes and huffed out a long breath.

"Hello?" Luther called out.

"I'm still shaken up about everything."

"I completely understand. I can only imagine what you are going through right now. Is there anything I can do?"

"Seriously? You literally called me out of my name and started a fistfight with Ayzo yesterday."

Luther took a sharp breath when I said Ayzo's name. "You know what? Yes, I was acting like a jealous dumbass, but can you blame me? I've had feelings for you since we were teens, and it bothers me that you didn't give me another chance. Then I saw you with that son of a bitch, and it pissed me off. He straight up got his dick wet, then left your ass. He didn't even bother to explain himself, but then he popped back up, and here you are, spread leg for him."

I let out a disgusted scoff. "If not for you holding the note Ayzo left for me hostage, I would have known the truth about why he left that night. I would have gladly waited for him instead of hating his existence."

"I can explain."

"Fuck you, Luther!"

"Wait, baby, please. I am sorry. I want you in my life, can't you see that? It enrages me to see another man near you."

"You don't want me; you just want to fuck me. News flash, Luther, I am not your property. I don't belong to you."

"Don't you know I'd do anything for you? I would give you the world if you asked?"

"I'm sure that's the same line you are feeding your stalker girlfriend who's been harassing my phone."

"What? I don't have a girlfriend. Wait, someone has been bothering you?"

I scoffed. "Be fo'real Luther, like you don't know."

"I'm being dead serious. Who the fuck has been harassing you?"

My mouth became dry. Who was it if that psycho wasn't one of Luther's groupies?

"Denice?"

I shook my head. "Luther, I got to go. I don't have the energy for this."

"Baby, wait, please. I can and want to protect you. If you give me a chance, you can have everything your heart desires—you won't have to worry about that little business of yours anymore."

My blood boiled with anger. "How dare you! It's not just a 'little business' of mine. I poured my heart into Dee's Designs! It can't just be replaced with useless gifts you are offering."

"Yeah, but —"

"And why would I want the world? This place is corrupt and evil—I'm only passing through until I get to go to my real home. I don't conform to this temporary place."

"Here you go with that religious mumbo jumbo. Do you think some imaginary man in the sky gave me everything I have, Dee? No! I did what was necessary to get me where I am today. The money, the cars, the businesses, everything was because of me! That was my hard work, not his, so you can miss me with that bullshit. I'm my own god, and I want you by my side as we rule together."

Repulsion, rage, and pity swirled through my core. Luther was lost, and this god-like mindset would be his downfall. I wanted no part of it.

"Luther, I have to go."

"Baby?" a female voice echoed on the other end.

A faint thud and a whimper echoed before the call went silent. Luther said he had to take a call a few moments later but would text me later before he abruptly hung up.

Who was that? Was she okay? It sounded like she got hit with something, but I wasn't sure. I dropped my phone onto my lap and rested my head on the bed. I said I wanted the truth, and I got it, but it wasn't what I was expecting.

Luther hated Ayzo because of me. It didn't make sense if they were working together to take turns on me like I accused Ayzo of earlier.

I threw my arm over my eyes as tears streamed down my face. I was so tired. Tired of not knowing what was going on. Tired of people pestering me. Tired of the drama and bullshit. I didn't know what to do.

Chapter 28

Ayzo

I paced back and forth in the hospital parking lot, contemplating whether I wanted to leave or wait for Denice to come to her senses. She was talking recklessly. I had no idea where she had come up with the solution that me and Luther - of all people - were in cahoots together. Tsk.

"Uh, what are you doing out here?" a male voice asked.

I whirled around to see Nick and Ashlynn walking towards me, their faces painted with concerned expressions. Shit, I was so worked up that I didn't even recognize Nick's voice. I needed to calm down.

I stopped pacing and relaxed my demeanor as much as I could, but my hands still trembled with frustration. I must've been looking like a crazy person out here, mumbling to myself and aimlessly wandering.

"Well, um, Dee suggested that I give her space since she believes my ex-friend and I are using her and planning to take turns with her. Oh, wait, after I go ghost again, THEN the other guy will have dibs."

"What?" Ashlynn yelped in disbelief. "First of all, is she okay?"

I nodded.

"Thank God. Okay, let me talk to her. When Denice is stressed or overwhelmed, sometimes her thinking can get muddled."

Ashlynn patted Nick on the shoulder and walked into the hospital. I leaned against the hood of my car and dropped my head. How did a night full of passion turn into a damn nightmare? How could Denice think that I'd hurt her that way? Who the hell was the psycho calling her phone?

I shook my head in frustration as my mind rambled with questions. I need to get down to the bottom of this mess before my baby has another damn panic attack, and I'd end up in jail for stomping a muthafucka out.

"You got it, you got it bad," Nick started singing at the top of his lungs, breaking the silence. I slowly looked up at him and glared before we both burst out into laughter. "Ahh, how the tables have turned."

"Fuck you, bro."

"Don't worry, Ayzo. Ashlynn will help console her so that y'all can talk like rational adults. Until then, any ideas on what could have happened tonight at Dee's shop?"

"I don't know. There's an open investigation, but there may be a possibility of foul play."

"Really?"

"Yup. The fire chief said that lighter fluid or alcohol was used to cause the fire to spread faster. I may have an idea who may have done it."

"Who?" Nick questioned with pinched brows.

"It's a long story, but I'd rather tell all of you at once. Think it's safe to go up yet?"

"Safe enough that Denice won't immediately try to swing on you, but keep your distance."

I released a nervous chuckle before walking with Nick back into the hospital. A long silence fell between us before I finally cleared my throat and glanced at my friend.

"I saw your mom earlier."

He stiffened and balled his hands into fists. "And?"

"She looks well. She's been volunteering here – helping out those in positions similar to those she was in."

He grunted and mumbled a good for her under his breath. We made it to Denice's door before I stopped Nick.

"Look, man, I know what your mom has done to you and Garrett in the past, but I could see how much she's changed – or at least trying to."

Nick's jaw clenched as he leaned his back against the door. He didn't say anything, so I kept speaking.

"She also wanted to thank you for putting up with her bullshit for so long. She confessed to not being a mother towards you the right way, but she wants to at least try for you to not hate her as much." I shrugged, "It doesn't hurt to just hear her out."

Nick sighed and rested his head back on the wall. "Yeah, yeah, I know. My therapist said that I needed to open up to the idea of letting go of the hurt that she generated. It won't happen overnight, though."

"Baby steps, man." I gave him an encouraging smile before looking at the closed door to Denice's room.

"Just remember to duck if she picks up anything heavy," Nick instructed.

I flipped him off while smirking as I opened the door.

Chapter 29

Denice

I scowled at Ayzo as he and Nick slowly entered the room. Ashlynn leaned over and pinched my leg with a stern look.

"Ow!"

"Stop being cruel. I love you, but girl, after what you just told me, you were most definitely talking out of your ass." Ashlynn stated.

I rolled my eyes.

"Let's dial the belligerent attitude back for just one moment," Nick commented. "Dee, I'm glad you are safe, and don't worry, we'll get your shop back up and running in no time."

"Yeah, love, you scared me half to death when Ayzo called and said you were in the hospital. Nick and I dropped everything to get to you as fast as possible."

"Thanks. "I am so lucky to have you both in my life," I said, tears brimming. I quickly dabbed them away as Ashlynn squeezed my hand.

"Okay, Ayzo has to tell us something – go ahead, bro." Nick motioned toward his friend, who was stalking next to the door.

I reluctantly looked over at him as he shoved his hands in his pockets.

"The day I went into your office to grab that folder for your business meeting, I heard Jasmine and some man in the bathroom. I wasn't thinking anything of it until I heard him tell her not to worry about you and he'd handle everything. So, of course, I wanted to know what the fuck they two were plotting. So, yesterday, I snuck through Jasmine's backyard."

My eyebrows shot up to my hairline. Ayzo was the dog spying that infuriated the person harassing me.

"What did you do?" I blurted out.

"I didn't do anything, I swear. I saw Jasmine and Bobby fucking and plotting to steal money out of your business accounts and transfer it into theirs."

"Bobby?" Ashlynn shouted out.

"What the fuck?" Nick barked.

"Wait, they were trying to steal from me?"

We all began talking and asking questions as we tried to understand what Ayzo was telling us.

"Yes, Bobby's bitch ass was claiming that all of y'all stole from him even though he was the dumb ass that got fired.

Apparently, he went to Jasmine, started serenading her, and finally got her to agree to his plan. I heard them and had my cousin block your account, Denice. Only you can pull money out, and I have the special code to grant you that access."

My body eased a bit as I digested his words. I mean, the story didn't sound far-fetched, and Bobby would do some sneaky hoe shit like that to get back at Ashlynn.

Suddenly, my phone rang, and I jerked from the sound. Ayzo quickly walked to my side and glanced between me and the phone. I swallowed and nodded for him to answer. A startled look swept over his face before he quickly placed the call on speaker. The same raspy voice was on the line, giving a gut-churning laugh.

"Oh, come here, boy," the caller began kissing and clapping her hands as if she were calling for a pet. "Ayzo, that's a good boy running to Denice's rescue, but you were too late."

"I don't know who you are, but even worse, you don't know who I am and what I am capable of. I will find you, and when I do, you'll have hell to pay," Ayzo snarled.

"Oh, Akeno, I know exactly who you are. How's your cousin, Seojun? Is he still hiding out in Vegas like a scared little bitch?" the caller smacked their lips. "Don't worry, y'all will get what's coming to you."

Then, the call ended.

Chapter 30

Ayzo

After the doctor gave Denice her release paperwork, we decided to go to my Airbnb – it was the only place no one else knew about. Once we arrived, I ushered everyone inside and grabbed the hidden burner phone. I needed to contact my cousin ASAP and warn him that he needed to leave Vegas. I didn't know how they figured out who and where we were, but he wasn't safe there – not by himself, anyway.

I explained everything that had happened to my cousin, who agreed to hop on a plane and meet me in Philly first thing in the morning. It wasn't ideal since we still had no idea who had set him up back in Chicago, but we compromised that coming to Philly with me wouldn't stop his plan to get revenge. Besides, it was only temporary. I stepped back into the house to see everyone deep in thought in the living room.

"So," Ashlynn said, sitting upright on the couch, "what do we know? Do we have any ideas of who could be calling and harassing Dee?"

"My bet's still on Bobby," Denice mumbled before sipping her water. "He must have another female working for him too. We thought it was just my subordinate, but she died during the fire. They have been calling and harassing me for a week now."

"What the hell, Dee? This has been happening for a week, and you're just now saying something? I wish you would have told us sooner," Ashlynn bellowed.

"I didn't want you to worry, like what you are doing now."

"Well, hello! You were just released from the hospital. What if that would've been you pulling an all-nighter at your shop when the place got torched?"

"Lynn, baby, calm down. I get that you are worried about your friend, but working up her anxiety would not help us."

Ashlynn opened her mouth but quickly shut it before taking a breath and grabbing Denice's hand. She lightly squeezed, and they gave each other an apologetic look.

"What do we do? We can call the police, but they'll take their sweet time getting anything done." Denice asked defeatedly.

"I don't know you guys. I've known Bobby for over five years; he's not the sharpest tool in the shed. I mean, he's smart but more in a follower role than a leader. Someone else is the brains of this master plan, but who?" Ashlynn asked, drumming her fingers on her knees.

"What about his wife?" Denice asked.

"Charity?" Nick spoke out. "I mean, she was pretty pissed off with Bobby, not us."

"True, but what if she found out we were the ones to set them up to get thrown out of T's good graces? She may not have liked Bobby, but she had a cozy life and would've had a lot of money if Ashlynn had gone through with the wedding," Denice suggested.

"She has a point, "Ashlynn chimed in.

"I don't know for sure, but I'm going to figure it out," I said, grabbing my car keys.

"I'm coming with you." Nick jogged after me before kissing Ashlynn on the forehead. "You two stay here."

"What? Ayzo, you can't!" Denice ordered.

"Dee, let me do my creepy stalker shit for you, okay?"

She stormed up to me and attempted to take my keys, but I tossed them to Nick.

"Stop it, Akeno! I'm not worth all of this trouble."

"Yes, you are."

"No, I'm not!" She scowled before shoving me in the chest.

She slapped me across the cheek and shoved at me again and again, but I didn't move.

"What about now, huh? Am I really worth all of this drama?" Denice yelled, punching me in the shoulder.

I knew she was trying to get a rise out of me so I would get pissed off and storm away or leave her, but I didn't. I stood still, allowing her to let out her fear, grief, and frustrations. She had so much bottled up, and it would only be a matter of time before she erupted.

"I'm nothing but a ball of hurt and anger. I'll crack one day, and then I'll hurt you – just like how my dad hurt my mom! I'm just like him! Look how fast I snapped at you – how paranoid I was sounding with my accusations that you and Luther were trying to turn me out."

Tears fell down her face as she raised her hand to hit me again, but I seized her arm. I pulled her into one of the bedrooms, and she fell to her knees and sobbed. I knelt next to her and wrapped my arms around her body.

"Dee, you are not your parents," I whispered. "Yes, you are angry and hurt, but that doesn't mean you will turn into your dad. That doesn't mean you aren't worth real love. What you witnessed your dad do was not love. That was manipulation, anger, and irrationality. You have bottled up all that fear and anger deep inside for so long - it's time to let it go."

"I don't know how to love," Denice cried. "I'll do it wrong and will eventually push you away."

I maneuvered myself so that she was looking at me, and I began to wipe her tears. "Love is patient, and love is kind. You can't drive me away that easily."

I rubbed my thumb over her bottom lip before gently kissing her. She let out a soft whimper before wrapping her arms around my neck. Her body trembled as tears continued to stream down her face. I wanted nothing more than to show her how much I cared for her and that I'd do anything to protect her.

"Something is telling me to keep you close," I mumbled against her lips.

Denice's eyes widened as I repeated back the words she said to me all those years ago. Tears continued to fall down her face as she rested her forehead against mine.

"Then keep me close," she whispered.

Our kisses became desperate and hungry. Denice moved her hands down the front of my body and ran her hands up my shirt, dragging her nails across my chest and abs.

"Fill me up!" she demanded, pulling up her skirt. My mouth watered when I remembered she had no panties on. I had ripped them off her earlier; now they were in scatters somewhere in the main bedroom.

I licked my lips and watched as she bent over, allowing her ass to sit up in the air. A sly smile spread across her face as she watched my dick jump with excitement. She leaned farther down, resting her cheek on the carpeted floor. Her eyes were still on me as she spread her legs, giving me a full view of her juicy swollen cunt. She teasingly ran her hand up and down her sex, never breaking her eye contact. Her wetness instantly coated her fingers as she drove them inside of herself.

I growled and pulled her hips towards me as I slid my shaft up her pussy. I slowly inserted my dick into her opening, causing her to cry out. I gave her gentle, deliberate strokes that drove her to curse.

"Ayzo, fuck me harder!"

"Like this?"

I gradually thrust my dick into her deep and hard, causing her to buck underneath me. She moaned but shook her head.

"Faster, please."

"You're in charge, baby; I'll do whatever you want."

With that, I grabbed her hips tighter and drove my dick into her just like she wanted – harder and faster. I felt her pussy soak my entire shaft with each stroke I gave her.

"F-fuck," she groaned.

I pulled her hair, causing her head to rest against my chest. "You going to stop pushing me away?" I growled against her ear.

"Y-yes."

"Don't you know I'd do anything for you? I'd wait eight more years if that's what I have to do to prove that you can't shove me away," I said between gritted teeth.

Denice covered her mouth as her eyes began to roll, but I snatched her hand down.

"Oh, no, baby. I want to hear you moan."

The mixture of her pleasure-filled cries and her ass clapping back against me echoed throughout the room, motivating me to fuck her harder. I knew that Nick and Ashlynn could hear us, but I didn't give a damn.

"You're mine! Do you hear me?"

She frantically bobbed her head, but I gently yanked her hair.

"Let me hear you say it!"

"I'm yours, Akeno." She whimpered.

Her body began shaking, and I knew her orgasm was coming. I felt my balls tightening as I drove my dick into her again and again until we both let out an orgasmic cry.

We collapsed onto the floor and caught our breath. After a few moments, Denice sat up on her elbows and looked down at me. She ran her fingers through my coils as she smiled.

"You better come back."

"I promise."

I squeezed her lower back and kissed her before getting up. We fixed our clothes and headed back into the living room. Nick and Ashlynn weren't there but stepped out of one of the other bedrooms. I softly chuckled before pulling Denice to me and giving her one more kiss before nodding for Nick to follow me out the door.

Once we were outside, Nick chuckled and clapped me on the back. "I thought she didn't like you like that?"

I threw him the middle finger and laughed as we hopped into my rental car. I cared for Denice in a way that excited and yet scared me. She made me feel alive again, and I wanted nothing but to be a better man for her. I was only afraid because I didn't want to mess up.

I had a chance to prove how much she meant to me. I realized it wouldn't be easy getting through our past traumas, but I was willing to try. I knew Denice was afraid that either she or I could turn out like her dad, but it wouldn't happen. Denice may have pent-up wrath, but her heart was pure. If she can agree to go to therapy with me, then I know we'd be able to start our relationship fresh.

Chapter 31

Ayzo

I quickly glanced at Nicholas in the passenger seat, scrolling through news articles on the phone. He was worried that the tire shops would be next to be hit.

I cleared my throat. "Nick, I know I've kept a lot of secrets from you, especially about my past."

He clicked his phone off and gave me his undivided attention. "You sure have."

I took in a deep breath. I had a chance to start over with Denice and wanted to do the same with my best friend. So, I told him who Akeno Yi was. From living with my abusive mother to training to working as The Shadow to the day I met and left Denice, it all came out. It felt good talking to my best friend, who did not judge or criticize me for my past.

"So, you like a trained killer?" Nick asked, rubbing his beard.

I smirked, "Technically, but I've never taken it that far."

"Does Denice know?"

"Not everything. She knows about my mom and that I was The Shadow. I didn't fully detail everything I've done back then."

"Hmph. And the two years you had to go into hiding, what was that about?"

"My cousin, the one who took over the Jaguars, had gotten into some trouble, and I was the only one he trusted. The plan was to help him and be back in time to help you and Garrett with that drop."

Nick nodded in understanding. "I'm glad you weren't there," Nick stated while patting me on the back. He cleared his throat, "Where are we?"

"Jasmine Wells place, the girl that died in the fire. We might be able to find a clue or something here to lead us to who's been harassing everybody. If we come up short, then we'll take a stroll to Charity's place. Sit tight; I'm going to go open the door." I instructed.

I hopped out of the car and strode behind the rowhome like I did the other day. Thankfully, it was dark this time, and I could easily stay hidden in the shadows. I hopped over the fence and jimmied the lock on the back door. I kept the lights off as I trekked through the living room and to the front door.

I stepped outside to wave Nick inside, but a cold sweat broke out onto my skin. My heart raced as I dashed back to my car. He was gone. The passenger window had been smashed in, and a small splatter of blood was on the dashboard.

"You are one good hound dog," a sly female voice declared.

I spun around to see Kendra staring back at me. I balled my fists and began to charge for her when she held up the gun that was hiding behind her back.

"Aht, aht, I wouldn't do that if I were you. Wouldn't want poor Ashlynn and Denice all alone at your rental house, off of Third Street, up all night waiting for y'all." She said with a fake pout, an evil grin spreading across her face, turning my blood into ice.

"What do you want, Kendra?"

"We are going to take a ride back to your place and meet Bobby with the girls. Then we're going to grab Nick. Once we get what we want, we'll let yall go – easy as pie."

"You'd know that baking a pie from scratch isn't all that easy, but whatever. Let's go."

She laughed before her phone began to ring as she sat in the backseat directly behind me with the gun digging into my ribs. From the moment she pulled out the gun, I could've easily knocked it out of her hands, but I didn't want any harm to come to my friends.

"Hey, baby. Yes, I got him; we're on the way to pick up the two tramps."

She dug the gun into my side, anticipating that I was going to say something, but I kept my eyes forward. I controlled the rage inside, but Kendra and Bobby would pay when it was time to release it.

Chapter 32

Denice

"Girl, please stop pacing; you are making me nervous," Ashlynn complained as she sipped her third glass of wine.

Ayzo and Nick had been gone for over an hour, but neither was answering their phones. At first, I didn't think Lynn was as worried as I was until after her second glass, she grabbed the entire bottle of wine from the rack and put it next to her.

"Sorry," I mumbled, plopping on the couch beside her. "We need to take our minds off of the guys."

"How about we watch a movie? You know The Wood gets us cracking up every time." Lyn suggested in a chipper voice.

"Go Ro, go Ro, go Ro… that's my boyyy!" I quoted as Lynn started mimicking the scene from the movie. We burst into laughter, and my nerves eased up just a bit.

"Dee, whatever happened to that other guy that popped up out of the blue? You, oops, I mean your 'friend,' called L." She made air quotations as she emphasized the word friend, and I couldn't help but chuckle.

"I was being stubborn, don't judge me. As for L, which stands for Luther, he reminded me why I needed to stay far away from him. Girl, he kept threatening that I belonged to him and him only. Ayzo beat his ass yesterday, too, for calling me out of my name."

"Go Ayzo! I knew I would like him."

I beamed, feeling proud of my man. "He is very lickable. Oops, I mean likable."

Her eyes sparkled as a bright smile spread across her face. "About time you got the cobwebs dusted off that coochie."

"Lynn!" I yelped, holding my side from laughter.

"How was it?"

"I don't kiss and tell." I threw my hands up when she glared at me with slanted eyes. "Okay, okay. Girl! I think I almost cried from how good he had me feeling. He was nice when we were younger, you know, gentle, but now," I stopped to fan myself. "He was rough in all the right ways."

"Whew," Ashlynn exclaimed. "That's exactly how Nick be having me feeling. Swear those two going to have us feenin' for it soon."

"Soon? I'm mad we only had time for a quickie before he left."

We broke into a fit of laughter when there was a knock on the door. We stilled and eyed each other. I didn't think Ayzo would have forgotten his key.

"Maybe it's just a solicitor," Ashlynn whispered.

"This late at night?"

She shrugged, "I'm just saying. A cell phone company in my neighborhood had their sales rep walking door to door until about 8 p.m."

"I'll go check it out."

"Girl, no. Let them keep knocking – they'll get the hint when we don't answer."

I nodded, but the wrapping at the door increased after a few minutes. Whoever was there obviously wasn't leaving. I groaned.

"I'd rather tell them no now so they can skip this house in the future and stop knocking on the door, "I commented while standing up and stepping toward the door.

"Wait," Ashlynn demanded, dashing to the kitchen. She returned with the metal napkin holder next to the stove. I arched an eyebrow and smirked. "What? This thing is heavy and can knock a muthafucka out."

I quietly laughed and headed to the foyer to open the door. I skimmed the peephole, but a damn moth was in the way. From what I could tell, a man was standing on the porch with his back facing the door. I glanced over my shoulder and made eye contact with Ashlynn, who held the napkin holder high above her head, ready to strike. I took a deep breath and opened the door.

"Can I help you?" I asked, poking my head out.

The man spun around, but before I knew it, he kicked the door down, sending me flying to the floor. He raced in, but Ashlynn was ready. She swung her chosen weapon down on the back of his head, causing him to drop to the ground.

"What the fuck bitch?" he groaned.

"What the? Bobby?" Ashlynn yelled out.

"Surprise!' he sang, jumping back onto his feet. Ashlynn glared at him and attempted to strike him again when he pulled out a gun and pointed it at me. "Make another move, and your friend gets a bullet in her chest."

My mouth became dry as I stared into the barrel. Ashlynn put one hand up as she slowly dropped the napkin holder. "What do you want, Bobby?"

A devilish smile spread across his face as he licked his lips and eyed Ashlynn. "You know, I was instructed to bring you down to the warehouse, but I'm thinking about getting a bit of pussy before we go. It's been a while since I've had a taste of you, Lynn."

"Don't fucking touch her," I spat.

He cocked the gun and glared at me. "Did I ask you bitch? If I want to get my dick wet, then I will! As a matter of fact-"

Before I knew it, Bobby had charged towards Ashlynn and slapped the gun across her face. She fell, hitting her head against the floor with a thud, and didn't move.

"No!" I cried out, but he ran toward me and jammed his gun against my temple while grabbing a handful of my hair. My heart hammered against my chest as he unzipped his pants and pulled out his limp dick.

"Suck it!" he gritted between his teeth.

No, no, no! I refused to allow him to do this to me. My mind raced with different possibilities of getting out of this situation. I mean, I could bite him, but I didn't want his smelly ass dick anywhere near my mouth. I could punch him in the balls, but I didn't want him to shoot me or Ashlynn out of reflex. My eyes burned, and I squeezed them shut to hold back the tears attempting to escape.

"This feels like deja vu. That weak bitch Jasmine was in the same position that you are in now, except she didn't shut the fuck up crying. I had to tie her ass up just so that I could enjoy her tight cunt one last time. Do I need to tie you up too?"

I shook my head as my eyes widened, realizing what he did to Jasmine. He bound her up and left her in my warehouse, where she was burned alive. My heart ached for her – she must've been terrified.

"Y-you're the one who burned down my shop?"

"You shouldn't have had that light-skinned nigga spying on me. All we were going to do was take some money out of your account. Oh well!"

I cringed as Bobby let out a deep, low, maniacal laugh. I darted my eyes over to Ashlynn. She was still breathing, but blood was pouring out of her nose. I needed to get to her. I must save us, but how? I didn't want either of us to end up like poor Jasmine, but I didn't have a plan.

"Don't make me tell you twice," Bobby growled, pulling my head closer to him.

He briefly let go of my hair to yank up my white shirt exposing the mounds of my breasts poking out of my bra. He grazed his finger over them as he yanked on his length. I wanted to vomit. Oh God, please help me.

Just then, tires screeched in the driveway, causing Bobby to curse under his breath and walk toward the window. I scrambled toward Ashlynn, yanking my shirt back down, and held her head in my arms.

"Damn it, she's early. Sorry, Dee, I can't play with you now, but don't worry, we can pick up where we left off once we get to the warehouse." Bobby winked before stuffing his dick back into his pants and strolling towards the front door.

"Fuck you," I spat out.

"I plan to."

Ice ran through my body, and I could feel the bile running up my throat. I needed to get me and Ashlynn out of here. I had no idea how sick of a bastard Bobby was. He spent years hiding the true monster inside of him, and I was grateful that Ashlynn broke up with his ass.

"Are they ready?" A familiar voice asked.

"Sort of. We got to carry Ashlynn's ass to the trunk – had to knock her big ass out."

"Ugh! Fine. Come here, boy!" The woman called out as she snapped her fingers.

I stared at the doorway and observed as Bobby came waltzing back in with the gun still pointing at me, Ayzo on his tail with Kendra behind him, a gun digging into his back.

"Well, well, well – how nice to see you again, Denice," Kendra smirked as she squeezed Ayzo's shoulder.

"Kendra? What the fuck are you doing?"

"Did you think y'all could ruin our plans and not have to pay for it?" she taunted. "Bobby, I need you to – nigga why are your pants unbuttoned? You were supposed to wait!"

"Calm down, I didn't do anything yet. Just wanted them to get an idea of what was to come," he laughed, zipping up his pants.

Ayzo's eyes bulged as he observed my disheveled hair and clothes. He grimaced as he looked down at Ashlynn before he balled his hands into tight fists. Ayzo's jaw clenched as he snapped his eyes towards Bobby.

"What the fuck are you looking at?" Bobby barked, pointing the gun at Ayzo's head.

Ayzo's concerned expression instantly changed into something deadly. His face was frozen into a scowl, and his lips were clamped tightly, but he didn't utter a word. He just stood there glaring at Bobby.

"Put her in the trunk. Once you're done, tie her ass up." Kendra instructed Ayzo, tossing him some zip ties. When he didn't move, she pointed the gun toward me.

Ayzo's jaw clenched, but he did as he was told. He tied Ashlynn up and threw her over his shoulders before carrying her outside. He quickly returned and yanked me up onto my feet. He jerked my hands behind my back with enough force to have me about to curse his ass out. I knew we were in danger, but this cold, nonchalant demeanor he'd suddenly taken on was confusing me. Did he only care about himself? Where was Nick?

Before I could protest, he gently ran his finger up my forearm as he slowly began tying up my hands. He briefly rested his forehead on the back of my head. Long enough for me to relax, signaling that he was still with me, and quick enough for Bobby or Kendra not to notice. I clamped my eyes shut and inwardly exhaled. He had a plan, but I needed to keep my head on straight and follow his lead.

He tugged at my hands, ensuring I could not get out before he grabbed me by the back of my thighs and tossed me over his shoulder. Adrenaline pumped through me as I was carried out the door. How was Ayzo able to stay so calm? Then I remembered what he told me about being The Shadow. This type of situation must not have been new to him. I was scared, but I trusted that he'd keep us safe.

Once we got to the car, he sat me back on my feet and cut off the zip tie. I rubbed my wrist briefly before he gently rebounded them in front of me, allowing me to sit comfortably in the backseat.

"All we have to do is get to Nick, and then, I'll take care of both of them," Ayzo mumbled under his breath as he placed my bound feet into the car and gently squeezed my calf. I kept my face straight ahead and discreetly dipped my chin when I saw Bobby and Kendra strolling out of the house.

"Let's go have some fun," Bobby snickered with a menacing grin.

I hope Ayzo fucked him up first.

Chapter 33

Ayzo

I was going to tear these two muthafuckas apart as soon as I confirmed that Nick was safe. If I acted out too early, they wouldn't have said a word about where they took him, so I had to follow along.

The moment I saw Ashlynn on the ground bleeding and Denice's tear-filled face and messy shirt, it took everything in me not to throw that plan out of the window and rip Bobby's head off. He hurt Ashlynn and attempted to hurt Denice; he was dead.

"Turn right," Kendra instructed from the backseat.

We had been driving for forty-five minutes and finally made it to an old warehouse just outside the city. Its weathered exterior had faded brick walls, and the metal was beginning to corrode.

There were a few boarded windows, and graffiti sprayed everywhere with recognizable markings that I couldn't put my finger on.

I gathered Ashlynn from the trunk. Thankfully, she was still asleep, and the bleeding had stopped. I needed to get her to a hospital to make sure she didn't have any head injuries soon. Kendra pulled out a pocket knife and cut off the ties from Denice's feet but warned her not to do anything stupid before motioning her to follow.

My heart drummed against my chest as a mixture of anxiety and adrenaline washed over me. I remember feeling like this every time I was headed to do a job as The Shadow. The rush had butterflies swimming in my core and my pulse quickening, but I kept my breathing even. One false move, and we'd be fucked.

We stepped inside the warehouse, and the thick air instantly overwhelmed my nose with the musty smell of aged dust and decay. The lingering odor of death had my stomach churning, but I took slow breaths through my mouth. It was completely quiet, with the exception of distant dripping water and slow, heavy breathing.

I squinted my eyes until we made it to an open space. Nick was tied up in a chair that was in the middle of the room, tape covering his mouth. Blood poured from the side of his head and nose, his chest slowly rising and falling, indicating he was still alive. My blood boiled with anger.

"Hey," Kendra shouted, shaking Nick's shoulders. "Wake up! I brought you company."

He groaned and gradually picked his head up. Nick blinked a few times, allowing his sight to adjust to the light. His nostrils flared as his eyes darted between us. Nick gave me a questioning stare. I knew what he was asking without having to say a word. I slightly pivoted so he could see Ashlynn's profile. Rage brimmed his eyes as he noticed the dried blood under her nose. He began thrashing, attempting to break away from his restraints.

"Tsk, tsk!" a low voice echoed from somewhere in the shadows of the warehouse.

Nick looked over his shoulder and immediately froze. I followed his gaze and saw T sitting in the corner of the room. Of course! The markings were from T's small territory group, The Cobra's. He was gradually taking over more and more areas throughout Philly, recruiting multiple people to join his crowd.

Kendra walked over to him and planted a long kiss on his lips as she handed him her gun.

"Ayzo, be a good dog and tie that bitch up on Nick's lap. Since they want to be together, they can die together. Denice, you sit in the chair to the left." Kendra ordered as she sat down on T's lap.

I glared between the trio and contemplated how to get us out of this. I could've easily knocked Bobby and Kendra's ass out, but with T here, it was going to be more of a challenge. He had no problem pulling the trigger on anyone in his way, and there was no telling how many of his hired men were currently with him. I needed one of them distracted just long enough to get my hands on a gun so that I could take him out. I highly doubt Bobby or Kendra had the guts to shoot.

Keeping my face neutral, I did as I was told. I gently set Ashlynn down on Nick's lap and tied one arm around his neck and the other down the chair so she wouldn't fall. I locked eyes with Nick and hoped he understood that I would somehow get us to safety.

Denice began walking towards the chair when Bobby caught her arm and yanked her back towards him.

"I want to start with her."

Kendra rolled her eyes and scoffed. "Would you stop thinking with your dick for two damn minutes! You're the reason we had to kill that damn Jasmine girl before we could get the money. I swear pussy turns you into a fucking dumbass."

"The fuck did you say to me, hoe?" Bobby hissed, letting go of Denice's arm. "You know, T and I have been getting real tired of your mouth. The only role you and that mouth of yours were supposed to play in was to have it wrapped around one of our dicks. That's it."

Kendra glowered. "What the fuck are you talking about? I've been a part of the plan since they threw your ass out of Jill's, and you got fired."

"And what did you have to do to convince T to go along with our scheme?"

She opened her mouth but then quickly shut it. Her hands shook with frustration and disdain as she stood from T's lap. "So that's all I'm good for? Getting everyone's dick milked?"

"Kendra, baby," Bobby taunted, "that's not all you're good for. You know how to cook the hell out of some noodles."

"Enough!" T demanded with irritation. He stood from his chair and walked past Kendra. "Bobby, we need to handle good ole' Nicholas and Ayzo first, then we can discuss what's to be done with the ladies."

My stomach dropped as a sly look formed across T's lips. He lazily ran a hand down Ashlynn's face, causing Nick to jerk in his seat and huff out a stream of muffled curses.

T grabbed a handful of Nick's hair and yanked his head back. I took a step toward him when Bobby grazed the gun across Denice's face.

"You should've thought about that before you butted in my cozy setup at We Got Tires. Bobby was bringing in quite a bit of money for us, and if he had married Ashlynn, we would have all the shops reselling our 'used' parts, but no, you ruined it by fucking her." T snarled before letting go of his head. He then reared his hand back and punched Nick.

"You were selling stolen parts, you son of a bitch," I barked.

T gave me a bored look before snapping his fingers. I started for him, but suddenly, a sharp pain radiated from the back of my head. My knees gave out with the realization that I had been struck. I tried to stay upright, but a second blow came, causing me to fall over.

Bobby hovered over me with his gun as I passed out.

Chapter 34

Denice

My scream got trapped in my throat as Ayzo's body dropped to the ground. Bobby looked over his shoulder at me as he licked his lips. Hell no! I wasn't about to let that muthafucka touch me.

"You know, sometimes I fantasized what it'd be like with fucking both you and Ashlynn at the same time. Ashlynn was adorable and obedient, while you were stunning and dominant. The perfect duo." Bobby reached down and grabbed his dick as he strolled toward me.

"You're fucking sick." I snarled, taking steps back.

"Bobby!" T snapped. "Only Ashlynn, remember? Do what you want with her, but Denice cannot be harmed. Not yet."

A sinister grin formed on Bobby's face as he turned to face T, pointing his gun at him. "Fuck you! I want them both."

"What about your cut of the money?" Kendra asked, picking at her nails in boredom.

"Damn the money! I want all of them to suffer for what they did to me. I had to grovel and beg to get back into The Cobras like a pathetic loser. Shit, T, you wouldn't have let me speak to you if I hadn't convinced Kendra to suck you off."

"You're talking reckless, boy," T chuckled, looking down at Nick and Ashlynn. He ran his hand through Ashlynn's hair, causing Nick to let out a low growl.

"You owe me! I was the one to get that dumb Jasmine girl to turn on Denice and get all of the information on her business accounts. I was the one who had to put up with Ashlynn for years and had money flowing in your pockets." Bobby snarled.

T smirked before sighing. "I suppose you're right. If you don't want your half of the money and would rather get your revenge, then so be it. I can't tell a grown man what to do." T waved a hand before turning his back.

The pounding in my ears drowned out the rest of the world as Bobby quickly turned and charged toward me. What the fuck? He was so furious and vengeful about losing his job and position within T's little group that he was willing to fuck up their plans just to get back at us. T nor Kendra made an attempt to stop him. There was no escaping Bobby's wrath.

I allowed my tears to fall, the burning sensation warming my cheeks. I couldn't fight or outrun all three of them. I mean, I could get a few kicks in, but that was about it. Ayzo and Ashlynn were passed out, and Nick was tied up. It was only me left. How could I save all of us?

I flared my nostrils and squared my shoulders as a plan crossed my mind. I'll have to allow Bobby to have his way with me, but only for a bit. Once he was in a vulnerable position, I could attack. It wasn't the best idea, but it was the only one that could give me a saving chance. I knew Bobby had tucked his gun in the front of his waistband. I could arouse and distract him enough to take it.

"Now, where were we?" Bobby hissed, grabbing the back of my hair and yanking me to him. He pulled my face to the side, and the mixture of his hot breath and wet mouth made my stomach churn as he dragged his tongue up my cheek.

I groaned in disgust. I swallowed down the bile and clamped my eyes closed as Bobby bit down on my neck.

"I only have to deal with this for a little bit longer. Once I got my hand on the gun, I was going to fuck up his world," I thought to myself.

Suddenly, Bobby's hand tightened, burning my scalp. His body stiffened, and his breaths became labored. I slowly turned to see Kendra resting her chin on his shoulder, one hand on his chest and the other behind Bobby's back. Little by little, a menacing smile swelled across her face as she kept her eyes on me.

"You're a worthless piece of shit," Kendra whispered into Bobby's ear as she pushed her shoulders in a twisting motion.

Bobby's eyes protruded, and his face contorted as she yanked her hand back and plunged it into his back two more times. The movement reminded me of how my dad did the same to my mother. Bile rose in my throat as Bobby dropped to his knees. The crimson-stained pocketknife sticking out of his back and Kendra's hand covered in blood caused me to whirl around and vomit.

"The fuck," he groaned, blood trickling from his lips.

"Kendra isn't just good for sucking the cum out of my dick, even though she's great at it," I heard T laugh.

I wiped my mouth and turned back to see Kendra glaring at me. Nick jostled in his seat before T squeezed his shoulder, causing him to wince.

"You see, Bobby," T continued, "Kendra actually isn't afraid to do the work. She noticed how reckless you are when pussy is involved. As you mentioned, you have done great work for me in the past and have made me a lot of money. So naturally, I thought she was tripping. But now, I see that I was wrong. You're a liability that I am not willing to risk."

Bobby coughed out a gargled fuck you. T smirked.

"Kendra, knock Denice's ass out so we can get out of here. I'll get my men out here to carry her to the car, and we'll burn this place down."

"With pleasure," she sneered. "Remember when you decided to ambush me at my job? Payback's a bitch."

Kendra drew her hand back and hit my temple with the blunt of the knife. My vision blurred as a flash of white took over my sight. Blinding pain tore through my skull as I hit the ground, my eyes fluttering closed. I wanted to scream out in agony, but I lay still.

Allowing my breathing to slow and my body to relax, I listened as Kendra huffed a satisfying breath before walking away. She thought she had knocked me unconscious, but by the grace of God, I wasn't. This was my chance to get us out. Their footsteps became faint in the distance, and I waited until I heard a door open and close.

I popped my eyes open and slowly sat up. My head throbbed with pain, but I couldn't think about that right now. I only had minutes before T and Kendra came back. I made a mental note to thank my self-defense coach when we were safe again.

I swiftly moved toward Bobby and yanked the knife from his back. He shrieked and tried to reach for me, but I kicked at his hand. I turned to head towards Nick when Bobby grabbed my ankles and hauled me towards him. I fell, feeling a sharp pain race down my body as my chin slapped the ground. My teeth clattered, and I swore one of them was loose now.

Thinking quickly, I reared my foot back and stomped him in the face as hard as I could. The crunching sound of his nose filled the room, followed by his head smacking against the concrete. Blood spilled from his skull as his eyes rolled in the back of his head.

I trembled and felt my stomach churn at the sight. I shook my head, straining to get the bone cracking out of my ears, but it was useless.

I glimpsed down to see Bobby's eyes fluttering closed as he continued to bleed out. I leaned to my side and dry heaved. I clamped my eyes closed and breathed through my nostrils. I could hear Nick's frantic muffles as he pulled at his restraints, reminding me I had to keep moving.

I exhaled before scrambling to my feet and dashing toward Nick. My head spun, and I wanted to sit down to control the dizzy spell, but if I stopped moving, then we'd all be dead. I finally made it to Nick and walked behind the chair, placing the butt of the knife in his hands.

"Hold it tightly," I instructed as I began sawing at the zip ties around my wrists.

My hands became free, and I promptly released Nick and Ashlynn before racing to Ayzo.

"Wake up, baby," I demanded, gently shaking his shoulder.

"Lynn, come on, baby girl," Nick whispered, running his hands down her face. Ashlynn stirred before opening her eyes and moaning in pain.

"Nick?"

"Thank God, you're okay. Don't worry; we're about to get out of here," he promised, rubbing her back before assisting her to her feet.

I continued to shake Ayzo until he woke up. He groaned and rubbed the back of his head.

"There you are," I cooed, planting a quick kiss on his forehead. "Come on, we got to get out of here."

Nick rushed over and helped me get Ayzo back onto his feet. I hurriedly snatched the gun out of Bobby's waistband before instructing everyone to follow me out of the building. I had no idea when T and his goons would return, but I didn't want us to stick around to find out.

We all ran out of the warehouse and back to the car, where, thankfully, Ayzo still had the keys. He dug under his seat and handed me a burner phone as we piled in. Ayzo stepped on the gas, causing the tires to peel out, and I called the police.

"Bitch!" I heard Kendra screaming as she came running out of the warehouse with two of T's men. They pointed their guns and started shooting at us.

"Hold tight!" Ayzo demanded as he sped up.

Bullets bounced off the car's trunk, but Ayzo had us back on the main road- out of their reach.

Chapter 35

Denice

I spent hours in a secluded office at the hospital, giving my statement to the police and recounting the events of the night. Ashlynn, Nick, and Ayzo were being examined by doctors to ensure they were okay to be released.

The doctors had already examined me, and thank God, I was alright. Well, besides losing one of my bottom front teeth after hitting the concrete, I had no other damage. It all seemed so surreal like I was dreaming, but the cold metal chair I was sitting on reminded me that I was very much awake.

A knock came at the door, and the two officers, Jenkins and O'Conner, stepped in.

"Can I go check on my family?" I asked, rubbing the bridge of my nose. We had all already given our statements about what had happened tonight, and I was ready to go.

"I'm sorry for the long process, Ms. Hintson. We have a quick update for you, and you are free to go," Officer Jenkins stated, sitting next to me. She was an older black woman, probably in her late forties, with short black hair and smooth chocolate skin.

"What's going on?"

"We have apprehended Kendra Williams, who is currently in our custody as a suspect. We caught her trying to cross state lines to New Jersey once we put out a 'person of interest' across all patrolling units. We will need you all to participate in a lineup. Bobby Robertson was pronounced deceased a half hour ago. He did not succumb from his wounds."

"And T?" I asked, feeling a mixture of sorrow and hopefulness.

"Terrence Mills is still wanted for questioning, but we've been after him for a while now. We cannot disclose confidential information, but rest assured his reign is ending," Office O'Connor declared.

The Caucasian male was younger than his partner, probably in his early thirties, with golden blonde hair and hazel green eyes.

"What am I supposed to do until then? Will protection be provided for me and my family? He tried to kill us!" I rambled out.

"Ms. Hintson, we completely understand your concern. We will have police officers in your vicinity as long as there is availability."

I stared between the two officers with disbelief. I knew they wouldn't help keep T or the people who worked for him away from us. We were pretty much on our own. I swallowed the lump in my throat and just gave them a simple nod. They handed me a copy of their cards. They instructed me to call if T contacted me or if anything else I could think of came into mind before I was released.

I followed as one of the nurses escorted me to everyone else's room. A part of me was relieved that Kendra was arrested and Bobby didn't make it. Not that I was happy he was dead, but at least I knew he couldn't bother us anymore.

My joy was shortly lived when the thought of T rushed to the front of my mind - we still had to deal with him. I'm not sure how or when he'd send more of his people after us, but I hoped that the police caught him before that could even happen.

"I'm so glad you are okay, baby," I heard Nick speak out. "I don't know what I would've done if I lost you."

I peeked around the corner to see Nick rubbing Ashlynn's arm as she rested her head on his shoulder on the hospital bed. Ayzo was staring out of the window, his hands jammed into his pockets. A look of worry was etched across his face as his nostrils flared.

"If anyone of y'all would have had any type of damage, Kendra and T would be in the morgue like Bobby." I quipped, folding my arms across my chest.

Ayzo snapped his head in my direction before rushing toward me and wrapping me in his arms.

"Are you okay?" He asked, examining me.

I chuckled before resting my head on his chest. "I'm fine, but glad that you are okay. When I saw all of you getting hurt, I was ready to knock all of their heads off."

"My little fighter," Ayzo teased, kissing the top of my head.

"Man, y'all should have seen Denice. She didn't panic or anything but stayed calm, cool, and collected."

"Oh, please, Nick. I was most definitely terrified," I argued.

"Well, you did a great job not displaying it. The way she pretended as if Kendra knocked her out and then stomped Bobby in the face – whew! If it wasn't for you, Denice, I don't know what would have happened to us - thank you." Nick stated, giving me a smile full of gratitude.

Ayzo gazed down at me before leaning down and passionately planting his lips on mine. "My hero! Did I mention that I loved a woman who takes charge?"

"Mhmm, you may have mentioned it," I chuckled against his lips.

He smiled before smashing his lips into mine again.

"Aww! Get a room," Ashlynn giggled.

"Alright, let's get out of here," Ayzo expressed, clutching my hand. He unexpectedly bent down and whispered in my ear, "I want to show you my full appreciation."

Chapter 36

Denice – 5 months later

I placed the last teal pillow on the miniature beige sectional couch and examined the lobby. Ashlynn's shop had come along beautifully, and I was excited for her to see all of Nick's hard work.

After we were all kidnapped and went through bullshit a few months ago, Nick didn't hesitate to get Ashlynn's salon started. He told me and Ayzo that he didn't want her to wait anymore for what she deserved. He hired the best contractors in the city and had Ashlynn's salon up within three months. I spent the following two months getting all the furniture and supplies she needed to stock up her shop.

In the midst of getting her salon in order, I was rebranding and remodeling my new warehouse and shop for Dee's Designs,

LLC. It surprised me how supportive and caring my clients were. No matter how much I told them not to, they came by to help clean up the debris or donated to rebuilding. I could feel my eyes burning with tears just thinking about how much I loved my clients and customers.

Of course, Ayzo, Ashlynn, and Nick were right by my side helping, too. I chuckled to myself at how many times we almost got caught by Ashlynn with getting both of our shops up and running. The furniture delivery got our addresses mixed up. I had to lie and convince Ashlynn that the furniture was a part of my catalog and not for her.

My smile faltered as a shiver ran up my spine. Even though Bobby was dead and Kendra was in jail, T was still missing. Yes, it had been quiet, and no one had tried to hurt or kidnap us, but still, we all kept our guards up. T was probably using this time to get more goons to hunt us down. Maybe he was waiting to catch us slipping before he attacked again.

"No, Dee! No negativity." I said out loud. I took slow, deep breaths like my therapist, and I practiced.

I had no idea if T was still out there, but I suspected we would be okay since we hadn't heard from him for this long. Hell, if he wanted to attack, he could have done it. The police stopped patrolling the tire shops, my shop, and our homes months ago, and we were returning to our lives.

"This place looks phenomenal!" Nick beamed, walking through the door

"You did a great job with the build!" I complimented, turning to face him.

"Eh, this place would just be a regular old building if you hadn't designed it. This place is fantastic!" Nick walked around, inspecting the completed project with a wide grin plastered on his face. "I couldn't have done this without you and Ayzo."

"Dee, baby girl, you did your thing with this salon. I'm going to need you to come and redecorate my apartment back in Cali," Ashlynn's granddad exclaimed, walking in behind Nick.

"Dad, me and Linda just repainted your apartment," Mr. Henderson, Ashlynn's dad, stated, walking into the salon. Right behind him was Ms. Linda, his long-time girlfriend, holding a pineapple upside-down cake - Lynn's favorite.

I laughed as I walked around and embraced everyone. Ashlynn's family took me in as if I were their blood. I loved them and was happy they made it down to celebrate Ashlynn.

"What time is that Aye-yo, A-kon, boy bringing my baby here?"

"Akon is a singer, Grandad." I snorted.

"Pops, I told you it's Akeno or Ayzo," Nick laughed. "They should be here any minute."

"And don't pop out of your hiding spot until you actually see Ashlynn," Mr. Henderson instructed his dad.

"Yeah, yeah. You're lucky I kept my mouth shut this damn long."

"They're coming!" Ms. Linda shrieked excitedly, peeking behind the front window curtains.

Nick quickly turned off the lights as we all hid. Granted, the salon didn't have too many hiding places, but she'd get the gist.

"Ayzo, why are we walking up to an abandoned building?" I heard Ashlynn ask, but my bae just ignored her as he opened the door.

"SURPRISE!" We all shouted while Nick flipped the lights on.

Lynn's Beauty hung up in neon lights illuminating the area. A station for shampooing and conditioning, blow drying, two areas for nail technicians, and three other salon chairs covered the left and right walls. Ashlynn's chair was in the middle back of the salon, positioned so that she could see anyone walking in without having to stop what she was doing. At the front of the room was a cozy lobby with a self-service beverage area and a bookshelf filled with donated books from the generous bookstore next door.

Tears welled in her eyes as she stood frozen, taking in the view. Before she could say anything, Nick slid down on one knee and presented her with the most gorgeous engagement ring I've ever seen.

"Ashlynn Shantell Henderson, will you marry me?"

It was hard for me to hold the phone steady as I recorded because my ass was ugly crying like a muthafucka. I was so happy for my friend. She started to cry harder as she bounced her head, accepting his proposal.

A firm, familiar hand wrapped around my waist and took the phone from me as I wiped my tears.

"I love, love," Ayzo whispered in my ear as he kissed my cheek. "Just like I love you."

My heart hammered as his words sunk in. Those simple words would have had me packing and heading for the hills in the past. What if he was just like my dad? The minute I became unhappy and wanted out of this situationship, would he become so obsessive that he would try to make me stay?

I rested my head against his chest and sighed. Who was I kidding? Ayzo had proven to me that he was clearly not like that. He was patient with me and stepped in to protect me numerous times. No part of Ayzo showed that he would harm me in any way. Hell, he was even going to therapy with me, helping me overcome my fears. There was no need for me to keep running.

I shifted slightly and gazed into his eyes. "I love you too."

A wide smile spread across his lips before he leaned down and kissed me. I gladly accepted as I leaned into him. I was ready to start this new chapter.

Chapter 37

Luther

I held the phone as the automated message stated that I had a collect call from the Philadelphia County Jail. I blew out smoke as my finger hovered over the number two so that I could decline the call. I didn't want to deal with her ass, but I'd might as well get it over with.

"Fuck," I grumbled as I pressed the number one to accept the call.

"Luther, baby, I've missed you." Kendra's pathetic voice cried through the phone.

"What do you want, Kendra?"

A long silence fell over the phone, and I could tell she was surprised by my blunt hostility.

"L-Luther, what is going on? Are you okay?"

I scoffed. "I'm doing just great."

"You haven't written to me or visited! Why are you treating me like this? I did everything you asked and then some!"

"I don't know what the hell you're talking about." I shot back, rubbing the bridge of my nose. Her dumbass was on a recorded line – no way was she about to get me caught up.

"You said you'd take care of me!" Kendra cried.

I chuckled through the phone, "Bitch, please. I said what I needed so that you could spread your legs for me, but as easy as you are, I didn't even have to do all that. Now, stop calling my damn phone, you criminal."

She gasped loudly before I hung up the phone and sat it back on the table. I hadn't bothered to see her and barely answered the phone when she called, and yet, Kendra's ass was still trying to reach out to me. She got it in her head that I would bail her out.

I smirked; what a dumb hoe. I needed to get rid of her ass before she started running her mouth. Kendra almost unknowingly revealed my involvement with everything between Denice and the others over the phone. I couldn't allow that to happen again. Luckily, I was close to one of the guards at the jail. I was going to shut her up – permanently.

Yeah, so what I convinced her and Bobby to work together to get rid of Ashlynn and Nick for messing up my uncle's business. I gave them a straightforward job, but they fucked it up. Now Bobby's dumbass was dead, and Kendra's dumbass was locked up.

I was on a fast-track plan to have We Got Tires on our payroll permanently, which would have allowed my Uncle T to finally hand over The Cobras to me. I proved how valuable and powerful I was in Chicago, and I was ready to take charge and run these territories through the Midwest all the way to the East Coast, but I didn't want to do it without Denice by my side.

I was telling Denice the truth when I said that I had mad feelings for her since we were teens. Her shit-talking, sarcastic, and playful attitude was a major turn-on. She wasn't like all the other girls who let me easily run through them. Nope. She didn't take any shit, and she was pure. Nobody had touched her, and I wanted to be the first.

I smashed my hand down on my desk. If those two idiots had stuck with the plan, Denice would be right here with me instead of with that bitch nigga Ayzo. Nick and Ashlynn would be sinking at the bottom of a lake, while We Got Tires would be mine.

"Are you okay, daddy?" Sandy asked, lifting her head from my lap.

I gazed down at the fading purple bruise around her eye and shook my head, forcing her head back down on my dick. I felt bad for throwing my stapler at her face, but her dumbass had walked in when I was on the phone with Denice. I had to check on my baby since she was in the hospital. Granted, I was the one who had her business burned down, but still, I was worried about her.

I closed my eyes and groaned as Sandy swirled her tongue around the base of my dick while my length filled up her mouth. If it weren't for her and Cindy, I wouldn't be as powerful as I am now. Because of them, I was able to recruit half the men who were once loyal to Seojun, the older leader of the Jaguars. They betrayed him, and now The Cobras almost fully dominated from Chicago to Philly.

Hell, he shouldn't have kicked them out for getting too old. I mean, I would've done the same thing since the customers in that massage parlor liked the girls to be legal but still look young. Sandy and Cindy were over twenty-five now, and that caused them to not make the same amount of money they used to. So, Seojun fired them.

Luckily for me, they ran into an old friend of mine who sent them in my direction. Their vengeance toward Seojun allowed me to get vital information that bought out the majority of his men and transferred them onto my payroll, which sent his ass into hiding. The Jaguars have been mine for the past two years, and now I was about to take over my uncle's area. I was this close to being the most powerful man.

A knock came at my door. I snapped my fingers at Cindy who was sitting on the couch waiting for her turn to please me, to open the door. She obeyed without a second thought.

"Since you are interrupting me, I hope you bring me good news." I glimpsed at my oldest friend, Xavier, who smirked back at me.

"Yup. We found him hiding in New York."

I clicked my tongue before rubbing my hand down the back of Sandy's head. "Uncle T tried to hide from me because he knows they fucked up. What a fool."

"Want me to handle him?"

I felt my stomach flutter, and my nut was coming soon. I waved my hand at Cindy and nodded toward Xavier. "No, X, thank you for your work. Let Cindy take care of you for all your hard work – I'll handle Uncle T."

He nodded before grasping Cindy's hand and allowing her to take him out of the room. I picked up the phone and dialed the first number in my favorites. I held on to the sides of Sandy's head and made her be still. I wanted to hear her voice when I came.

"Well, hello, stranger."

The sultry voice was like an extra tongue sliding down my balls. I thrust my dick down Sandy's throat.

"What do I owe -"

Thrust.

"This pleasant —"

I moaned and thrust harder.

"Surprise."

I came down Sandy's throat and cursed under my breath. "Fuck Olivia. Your voice always makes me cum so hard."

She chuckled. "It better. So, what do you need?"

I slapped my dick across Sandy's face and pushed her head away, motioning for her to get out. She bowed her head and immediately left.

"I'm sending some cargo out your way that needs to get lost in the desert."

"Ooh! I like it when you talk dirty like that. Do I get to play with this cargo before I get rid of it?"

I rubbed the knife tattoo on my neck as my dick hardened with the thought of Olivia pulling the trigger and shooting Nick for the first time while his brother lay on the ground dead.

I was supposed to shoot him, but Olivia wanted to have that honor. Since she told me about the drop Nicholas and Garrett were doing and how much it was worth, I couldn't say no. Besides, I loved it when she got her hands dirty for me and took care of unwanted baggage — shit turned me on.

"You damn right, baby," I said, lightening up a cigarette.

I could hear the devilish grin dragging across her face.

"Perfect."

This concludes They're Not Strangers, Book II of It's A Vibe Series. The crew will be back in the trilogy – Strangers No More.

Acknowledgments

Wow! I can't believe that I am back here writing this after only six months lol. Okay, let me get serious.

First and foremost, I would like to thank God for blessing me with all of the opportunities laid before me, especially with my books. I would have never thought that I would have not one but six published books.

Thank you to all the book baddies who have enjoyed the It's A Vibe Series and have shared/liked/reviewed the book. It amazes me how much love and support y'all have given me, and I love each and every one of y'all!

Thank you to previous indie authors who've shared their tips and advice on self-publishing. Without y'all, my manuscript would still be just an outline sitting on my desktop.

I hope you enjoyed it.

 God Bless!

About the Author

I'd like to take the time to introduce myself. My name is Jessica but as you can see, I write under the pen name J.D. Southwell. I was born and raised in DFW, TX and I've always enjoyed reading ever since I was a little girl. Unlike most kids growing up, I spent the majority of my time at my local library. I eventually found my love of Romance and Mystery books.

I started writing my own stories when I realized what I wanted to read hadn't been written yet. I started my self-publishing journey writing children's books. *(Amelia and Andrew Learn to Pray, Love One Another, and Don't Be Afraid,*

Grace)

Once I got the hang of self-publishing, I wrote and published my first book, *Dating is Ghetto*: an erotic anthology novella.

After a year, I wrote and published 40hrs With A Stranger. Now, six months later, Book II is here – They're Not Strangers!

I definitely plan on writing more and will venture out to other genres. (Did someone say Horror/Paranormal?)

If you've enjoyed this story, please leave me a review and share this story with a friend. Feel free to follow me on Instagram and/or Tiktok 😊

www.jbookcollections.com

email: jd.southwell@outlook.com

Instagram: @jdsouthwells

Tiktok: @jdsouthwell

Made in the USA
Columbia, SC
20 November 2024